The World of Glimpse

Written & Illustrated by Ellen Palestrant

To Pat,
Welcome to "The World of Glimpse!"
May there be much joy in your life's journey.
And may you continue to create...
Ellen Palestrant
January 2012

Copyright © 2012 by Ellen Palestrant

First Edition 2012

10 9 8 7 6 5 4 3 2 1

Library of Congress Control Number: 2011944185

ISBN: 978-0-9848852-0-6

Artwork © 2012 by Ellen Palestrant
www.EllenPalestrant.com
ep@reclaimyourcreativity.com

Cover and Interior Layout: The Printed Page, Phoenix, AZ

Printed in Canada

To

My grandchildren, Nola, Leila, and Gideon.

And to Nossi...always...always in my heart.

In Appreciation

I am immensely grateful to:

My son Laurence—who has lived with the persistent presence of this ever-evolving work in his life, and who, over the last six years, ensured in every way possible, that I would have the freedom to complete it. He constantly spurs me on with his enthusiastic and astute insights into *The World of Glimpse*, his visionary ideas, and his belief in this work and in me.

My son David—who, also, ever since childhood, has lived with the long process of the creation of this work, and, over the years, seen it metamorphose. Unwaveringly, he has respected my perceptions, my writing voice, and my imaginary worlds.

My family and my friends—both old and new—for their support and enthusiastic embrace of *The World of Glimpse.*

Acknowledgments

I thank the following people for their invaluable contributions during the various stages of the evolution and completion of this work:

Jill Glenn—my first friend in America—and what a generous and supportive friend you have been! I so appreciate your constant encouragement, insightful perspective, and intelligent, deep understanding of the world I have been creating over all these years. I am immensely grateful for all of this—and for the way you persistently urged me to paint the book myself.

Juanita Havill—a thoughtful and stimulating friend who has provided me with much-valued affirmation and editorial insights during the years that I have worked on this book.

Maryanne Kremer-Ames and Allen Ames (**Lyra**)—loyal, caring friends who have brought their beautiful music and generous spirits into my life—and into our collaborative performance for the debut of *The World of Glimpse*.

Barbara Katz—an exceptional artist who opened her studio and heart to me, shared her expertise, and enthusiastically recognized my own artistic path.

Lisa Liddy (**The Printed Page**)—a dependable professional and friend, who has worked with dedication to make this book print-ready.

Liz and Steve Dokken—considerate and gracious friends who generously arranged for the filming of the debut performance of *The World of Glimpse*.

A special thanks to...

    Ashley Lazarus (Film Producer)

    David Meth (Literary Agent)

for all I learned from both of you.

The

World

of

Glimpse

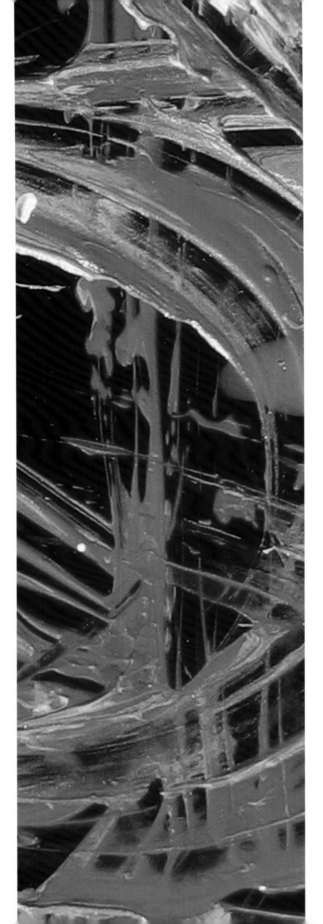

A
Glimpse

When Justgimious sat down to factulate in his new, red notebook on the morning of his one-hundred-and-fourth birthday, he found a small, red box on the table.

"A gift? Who could possibly have remembered?"

"Happy birthday, Justgimious!"

A rather ordinary-looking, yellow, wooden pencil jumped out of the box:

"Hello Justgimious...I am bright-leaded Fred."

"A talking pencil?" Justgimious examined it carefully. "A central core of sparkling lead with a perfectly sharpened point." Justgimious was particular about points—especially those he made on paper.

As soon as he began to write with his new pencil, he felt an unfamiliar surge of energy flow from his fingertips onto the paper. Lively letters vaulted excitedly across the page:

"I invite you to explore your imagination."

"I'm not interested in fiddle-faddle."

"Sometimes a bit of levity brings new insights."

"I wouldn't know how to begin."

"With a glimpse. Try to capture something fleeting. If you penetrate a glimpse, you never know what you might see."

"But I only record facts," said Justgimious. "I'm a factulator—not a fabricator. That's what I've always done."

"I will help you. As impressively productive as you've been, Justgimious, you're too earthbound. Did you know that stories often become facts?"

"Some might. But I prefer working with established facts."

"Just try to use your imagination, Justgimious. You might even create a whole new world. Of course, you will include us both in your story."

"A new world? What would I call it?"

"It's your world, so it's up to you."

"Then there'll be no fiddle faddle."

"You do want to explore your imagination, don't you?"

"Well, yes," said Justgimious.

"So,...

Skedaddle

from your mind
all you know.

Some...

Fiddle-faddle

will unwind
your flow.

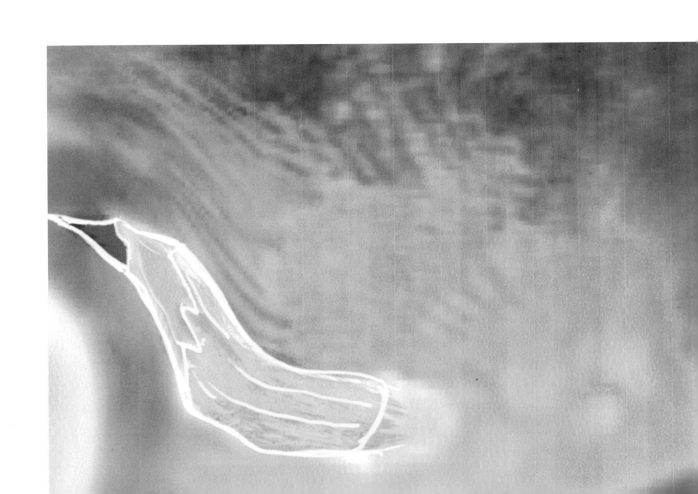

By...

Penetrating

a glimpse -

without intention,

you'll...

Step

into a world
from a new dimension.

If you...

shut

your eyes,

you'll hear some cosmic verse...
Songs and sounds of the Universe."

Sparks
of red
flashed
across the darkness.

More flashes followed, first orange,

then

yellow,

blue,

indigo,

and

violet....

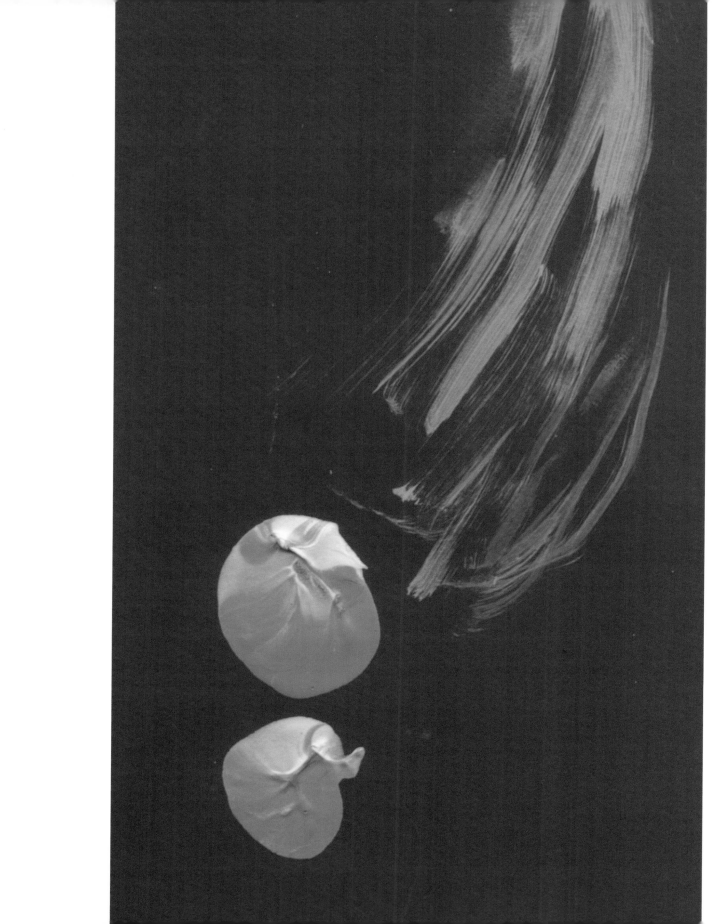

and then...

Justgimious heard a song:

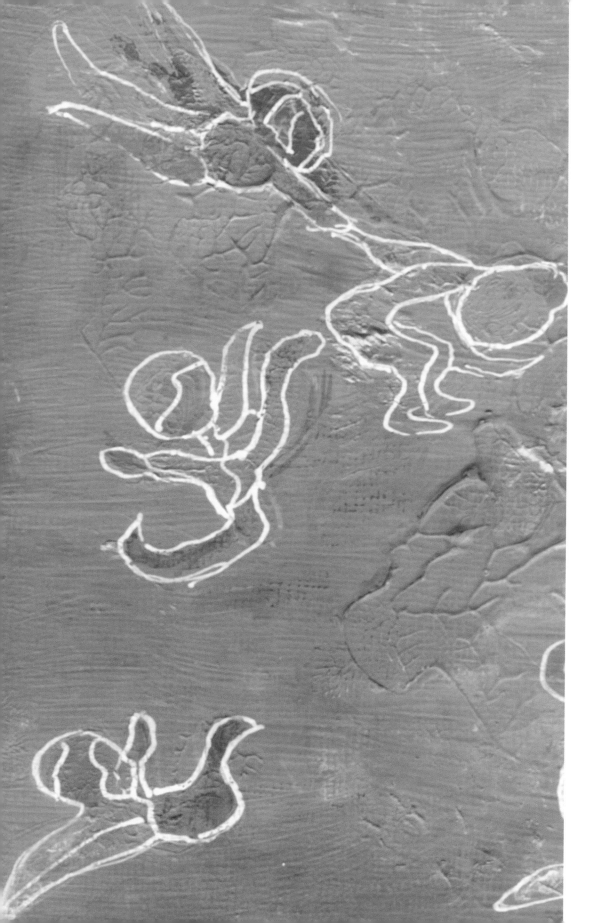

We are the Glimpsibles, flying through the sky,

spinning, twirling, whizzing up high.

Looking at Glimpse from another point of view,

seeing things differently, doing what we do.

We are the Glimpsibles having so much fun,

flying in a pink-blue sky with a turquoise sun.

Looking at our world from way up high,

looking at Glimpse from an any-colored sky.

Flat out we must race,

greased lightning right through space.

Flat out day and night

on a fantacosmic flight.

We zoom and zip, rapt in awe,

a wonder trip...

to worlds far and near,

we zoom in top gear.

We are the Glimpsibles having so much fun,

flying in a pink-blue sky with a turquoise sun.

Looking at Glimpse from way up high,

looking at our world from an any-colored sky.

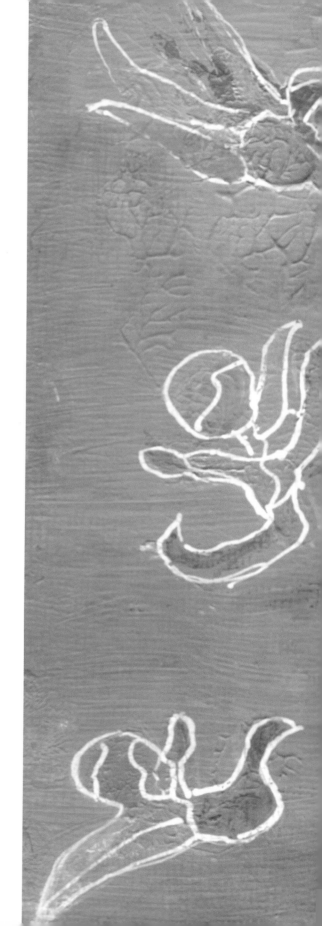

"I need to record this immediately!" said Justgimious.

And so, Justgimious (with the help of Fred) began chronicling a world: everything.
Its inception: a flash of color. Iridescent. More colors which mixed and matched.

He recorded images,
flutters,
fleeting shapes,
songs.

Wrote notes,
dreamed tales,
jumbled,
then tidied them again.

As thoughts and colors hurtled by, he captured them on paper, writing what he felt and saw...
while Fred flew off in tangents. The World of Glimpse unfolded, filling Justgimious' new notebook
with mixtures of his facts, and Fred's fancies...

Justgimious'
Notes

Glows, which light up the sky of Glimpse, emanate from the Glimpsible Sparks. These glows are the source of all color in Glimpse — all the colors that mix and match. When…

Justgimious-red

Farfetch-orange,

Perceptilly-yellow,

Zippity-blue,

Gumptious-indigo,

And Gregarious-violet

rainbow over Glimpse, every Glimpsible living under its arc feels almost safe from the dreaded Drooma of Sooma Sooma. One day, they'll feel completely safe when the seventh and last Glimpsible Spark is chosen because the rainbow will have a seventh color — green. One day, Glimpse will be entirely colored in, and the evil Drooma — those avaricious, color-sucking, spectroscopic parasites — will no longer be able to penetrate its color-tight alliance.

Now, who will become the last Spark of Glimpse?

1

An Any-Colored Sky

It was five-to-pink....

Spunktaneous flew high in the Any-Colored Sky as it changed from red to pink. In Glimpse, depending on the time of day or night, the sky could be any-colored. It also could have any luster. According to the transmission of a particular Glimpsible mood, it could glow as brightly as a new thought, or be as dull as dripe.

Spunktaneous flew higher...and higher. He felt part of the sky, part of the wind, and part of Glimpse, the iridescent, yet-to-be-completed color-world of the Glimpsibles. Because he was joyful, his sky glowed bright, shiny pink.

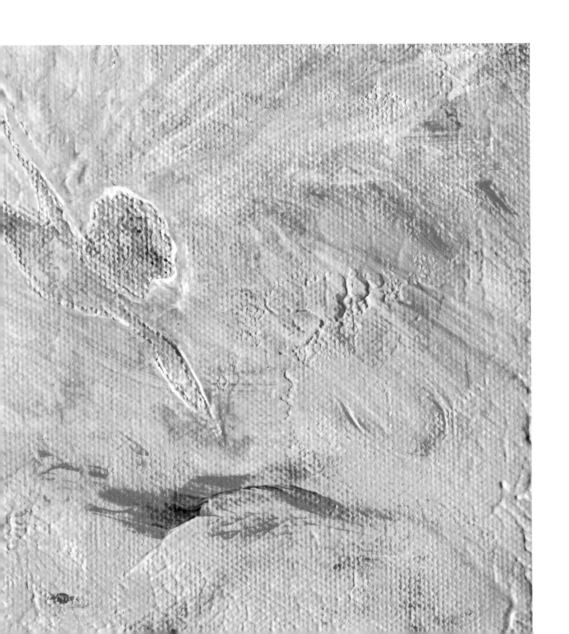

"Brighter than I've ever seen!" Spunktaneous shouted loudly, making sure that Justgimious, who was watching him from below, could hear him. "And pinker than my memory of pink. I see pink exactly as pink is now, and that's that, Justgimious."

"Colors are memories!" snapped Justgimious. "The only reason you discern shades of pink is because you already know them. I'm not interested in debating with you, Spunktaneous. I'm in a hurry. Come down quickly! I've something to tell you!"

But Spunktaneous didn't come down. He pretended he hadn't heard Justgimious. He was having far too much fun to come down. He juggled his juggling gems while doing somersaults, and flew higher and higher, faster and faster, round and round, up...up...up in the Any-Colored Sky of Glimpse,

twirling and whirling, spinning and turning,

looking at the world from

upside down,

inside out,

sideways and middleways,

under and over,

from topsy-turvy and bottoms-reversy.

Looking at the world from another point of view,

Looking at the world as Glimpsibles do...

"You have to admit that my pink is not the same as your pink." Spunktaneous continued to soar while Justgimious waited impatiently for him on the ground. "You have to concede, Justgimious, that my pink is my pink—entirely me. In fact, my pink might be pinker than your pink. You never know."

"I'm not prepared to engage in yet another numbdumb debate with you. Why do you always think you know everything? You have much to learn, Spunktaneous, and your verbosity far exceeds your ponderosity."

Justgimious felt his moodprint change. The glow of his sky began to fade

glot,

by glot,

by quite a lot,

by lots of glots...

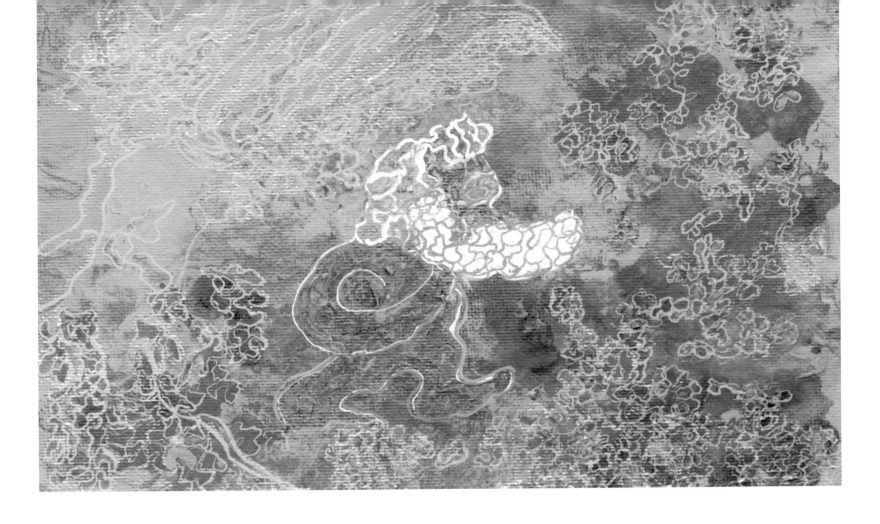

a glut of glots.

Justgimious, realizing that soon the dullness of his sky would reach glottonous proportions if he didn't alter his mood, made up his mind **not** to let Spunktaneous continue to affect him. His day had started luminous. That's the way he wanted it to end.

"Spunktaneous, come down now! **Concentrate** if you want to make a safe descent. I have good news for you—you've been chosen to visit the Rotundary."

When Spunktaneous heard the word chosen, he immediately started to descend. It didn't matter what he had been chosen for. He loved the idea of being

picked,

singled out,

selected,

even more than skymerging with the Any-Colored Sky of Glimpse, or feasting on Lunaberry Ice Cream which contained the flavors of all the best ice creams ever created and blended in the Universe. Being chosen was better than jumpalooning on the blue, marshmallow-soft grassy mounds in Lunaberry Forest, or bounce-walking on the quadruplequick...

with a rockwriggle rollabout swing-spring:

Spunktaneous could no longer concentrate as he descended. Thinking about one thing at a time was as unnatural for him as enjoying only vanilla ice cream. Just as a single spoonful of vanilla invariably led to a desire for dreamsoda or peppermintdust-wishes, so one thought led to forethought, morethought, afterthought, simulthoughts, and now, ponderthought: What was he being chosen for?

Lost in ponderthought, he never noticed the raindrops that had begun to fall, twistlanding softly on him. Nor did he notice the rainbow, which stretched-arched over Glimpse, shimmering

red, orange, yellow, blue, indigo

and violet ribbons

over Jumpaloon Mountains

and onto the Lake of Imaginings.

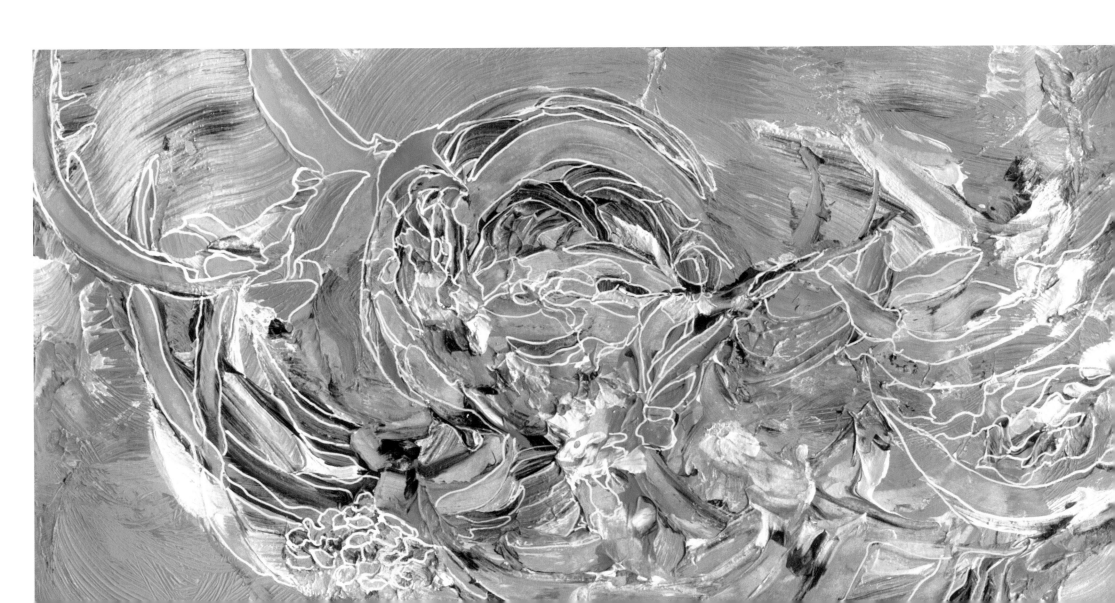

Ideas of what he might have been chosen to become, crammed his head, bursting through the borders of his thought-quarters...

"**Concentrate** Spunktaneous!" Justgimious shouted. "**Thinklink**!" But his warning came too late. Spunktaneous crash-landed through the trees right under Justgimious' nose.

"Wawawaoooooo!" Spunktaneous wailed a blusterous boohoo, sneezing the trees apart and shuddering the grass.

"Wawawaoooooooooooooooooooooooooooooooooooo"

echoed throughout Glimpse, caterwhirling the Lake of Imaginings into criss-cross, under-and-over currents which surged into the Phantasea....

dizzydazing the phantaphish

with their rocking, spinning motions,

and drenching the chimeroos,

the ellipops,

and the giroofs,

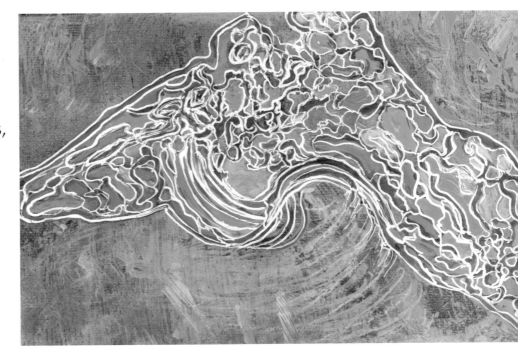

sunbathing on the shore.

What a hullabaloo! What a ballyhoo proceeded the final, giant, Glimpse-shattering...

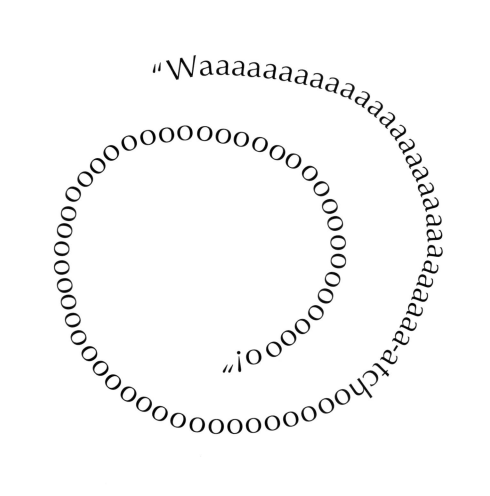

"Waaaaaaaaaaaaaaaaaaaaaaaa-atchoooooooooooooooooooooooooooooooi!"

Spunktaneous was mortified by his landing but still he asked Justgimious: "Chosen for what?"

Justgimious was too fed up with Spunktaneous to respond; instead, he marched off to his beloved Sagacity Bush deep within Lunaberry Forest. Seating himself beneath its branches, he inhaled its clarifying aroma.

Then he began to make notes in his **GLIMPSIBLE CHRONICLES:**

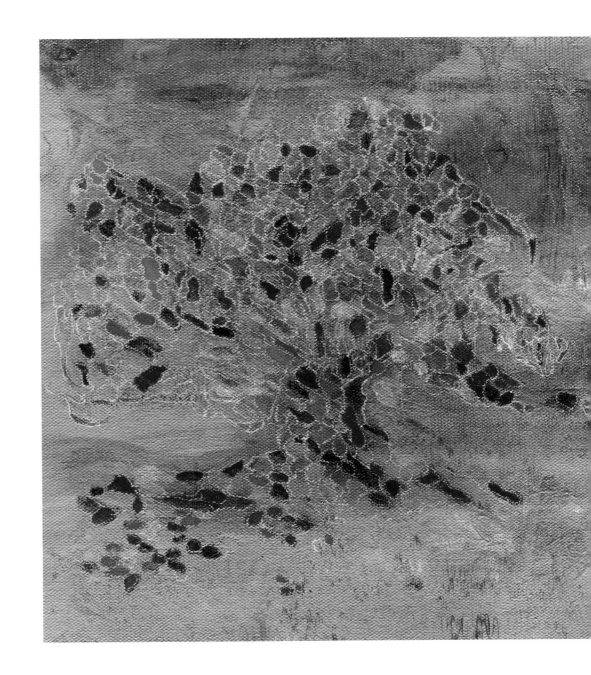

The search for the Seventh Spark of Glimpse continues. Spunktaneous' turn is next. He will have to complete his week in the Rotundary and be fully assessed, but…does he have that special sparkability?

Justgimious fell into a fitful sleep, worried, as always, that while he wasn't looking, Fred, would embellish his facts.

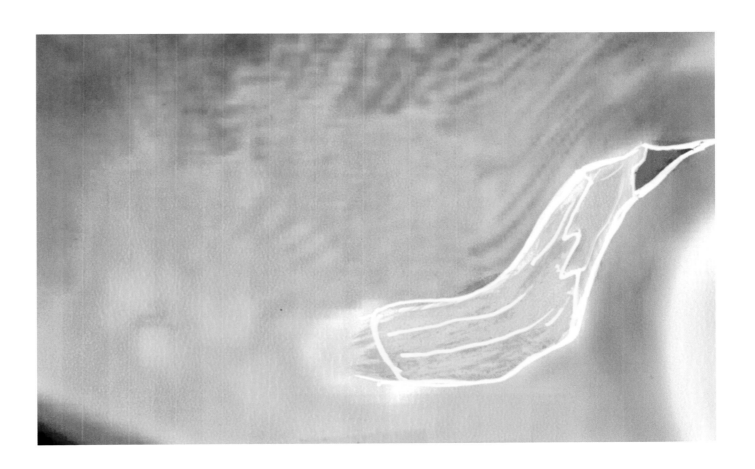

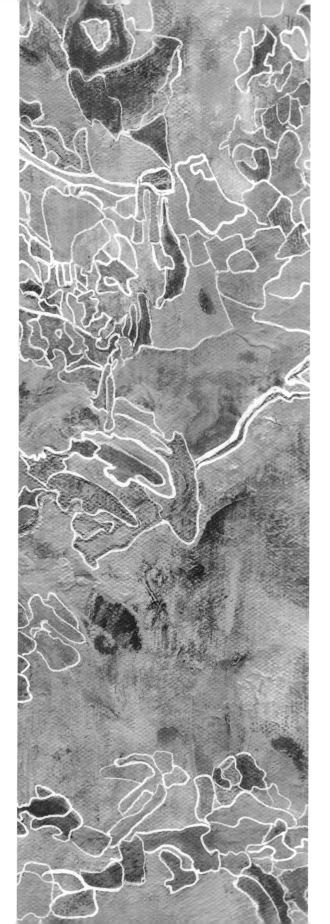

38

2

The
Rotundary

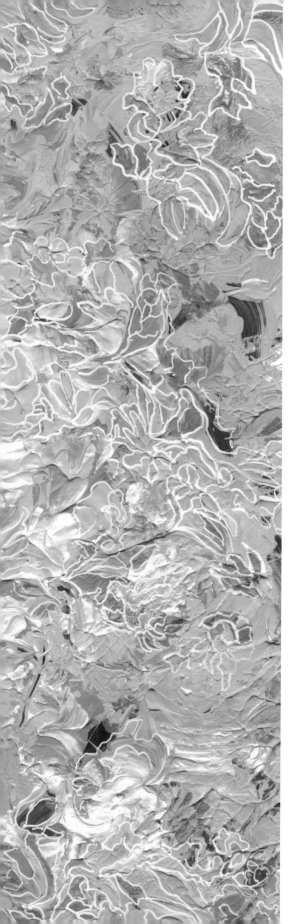

Spunktaneous tickled Justgimious' nose with a lunaberry blossom. "Did you say I'd been chosen?"

Justgimious jumped, trying to pretend that he hadn't been sleeping. He ignored Spunktaneous because, as usual, his moment of waking up was accompanied by a disturbing possibility:

"My Chronicles! Fred, did you change any of my facts?"

"Never touched them," Fred assured him. "Left them as always...dryasdust, mundanely matter-of-fact, and sooooo boring. Now if I were writing the The Glimpsible Chronicles, I would..."

"But you're not," Justgimious snapped. "You're just an annoyingly argumentative leadhead who should stick to pencilling what I ponder!"

"Justgimious—listen! My words could create..."

"Chaos and clutter! Just leave my words alone, Fred! I choose my own words."

Justgimious wrote in Fred's indelible, sparkling lead. Once written, his words (or any Fred had slipped in) could never be erased. They existed forever. Writing was as essential to Justgimious as breathing and certainly more necessary than sleeping. An exhausted Fred would often complain:

"I have writer's cramp...

and ...

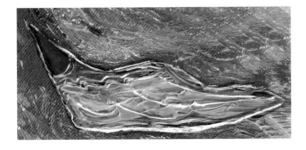

a lead-ache."

"Justgimious, you said I've been chosen?" Spunktaneous asked again.

"Chosen? Oh yes, to visit the Rotundary. But, perhaps, I was mistaken. Despite your emerging greenessence, I'm not sure you should be a candidate for Sparkhood. You're much too impetuous."

"My greenessence? **A Spark! Me?** Is that because I can soar higher than any other Glimpsible? And, while I soar, I can dazzle the sky with my sparkling jugglegems?"

"In order to become a Spark, Spunktaneous, you need to learn about the perfectabilities of the other Sparks as well as perfect your own—a lifelong pursuit. You will need to combine your perfectabilities with those of the other Sparks when necessary. Only one Spark will be chosen from all the candidates."

"When do I begin, Justgimious?"

"For the next five days, you will be apprenticed to each of the Sparks. Your apprenticeship will follow this order: The first day will be spent with Farfetch. The second with Perceptilly. Then the following days with Zippity, Gumptious and Gregarious. The sixth day will be spent at VERSEBLURT CAFÉ with all the Sparks — including me...

memorizing,   summarizing,

contextualizing,   crystallizing,

and socializing

with the other Sparks.

On the seventh day, you will rest, and that evening, I, Justgimious, the Founding Spark of Glimpse, will test you. If you pass, you'll be the seventh and last SPARK OF GLIMPSE.

"Imagine being a Spark!"

"Come Spunktaneous, it's time to go to the Rotundary."

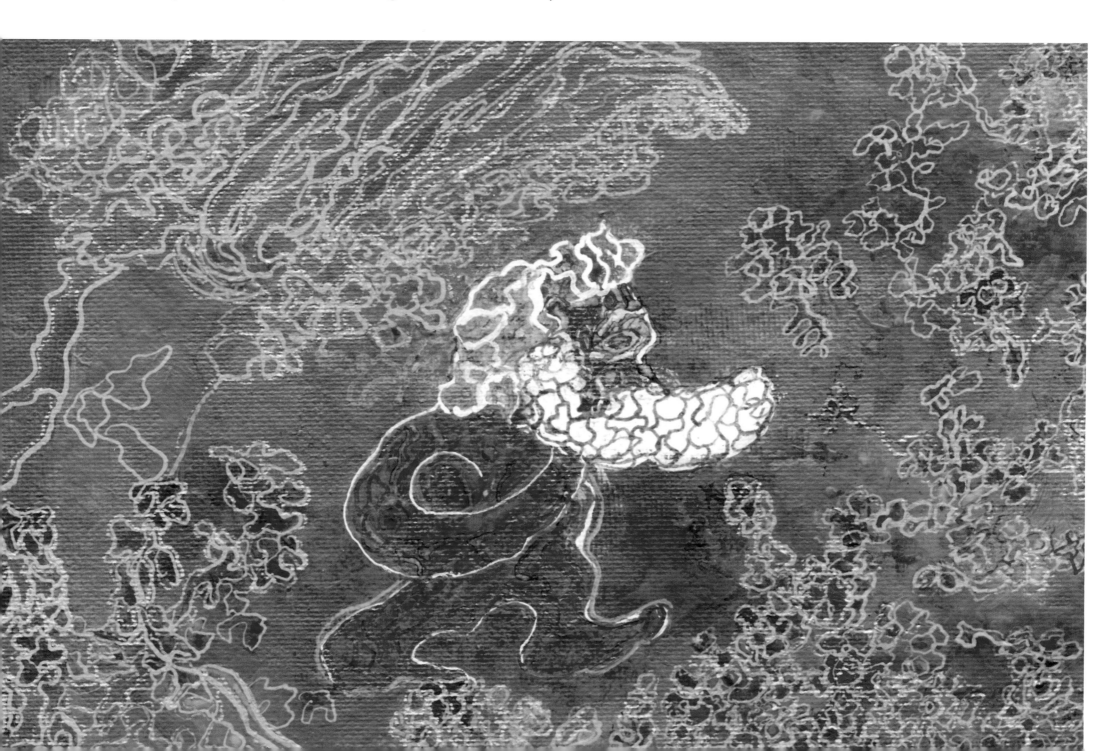

Spunktaneous eagerly
followed Justgimious.

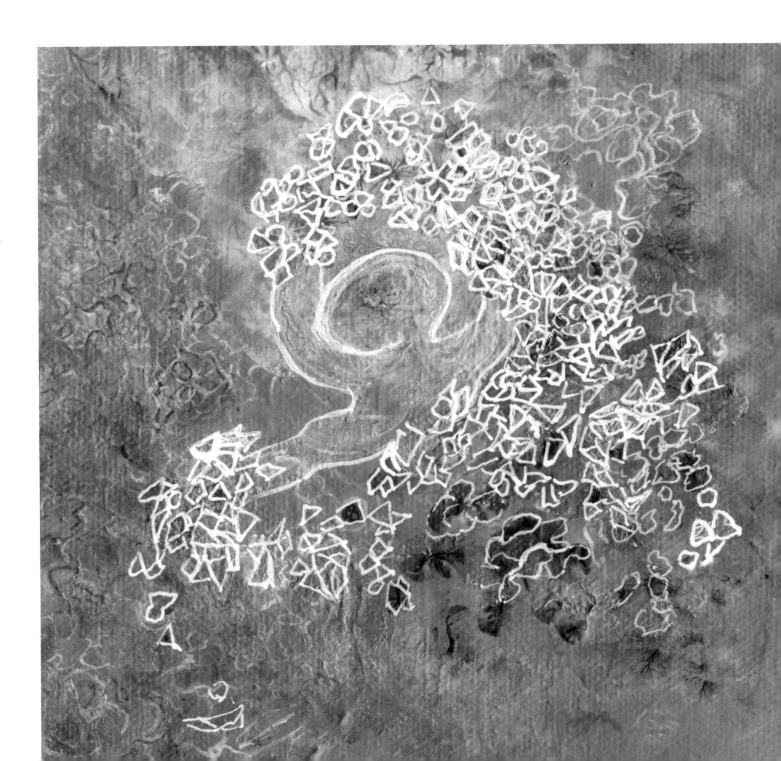

They passed Flutterby Center, the busy moth market with stalls clustered on either side of the street. These stalls belonged to the Lunaberry Moths who worked all day making everything a Glimpsible could want from what they had collected in the forest:

YARNSPINNERY SPECIALS...

Unique Mothtiques for special occasions.

Lunaberry Cloths—be invisible in all locations.

For anything
miscellaneous...
Come to
THE MOTHELLANEOUS.

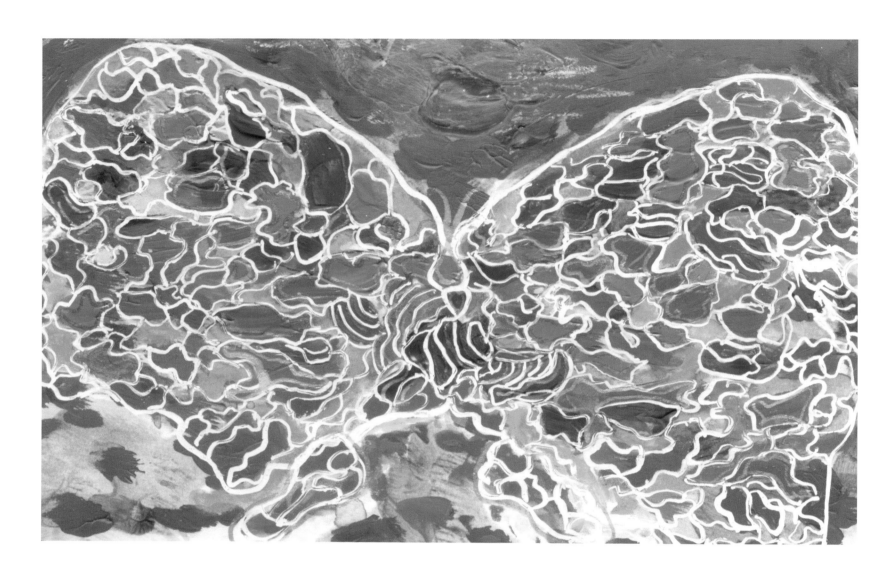

Sorted Specifics...

Available

Now at KWANTIFICS.

"Could we stop and look through a colorcollide?" Spunktaneous asked Justgimious as they passed a spherical glass stall. "Maybe one with purple perception, or a surge-merge into pink reflection?"

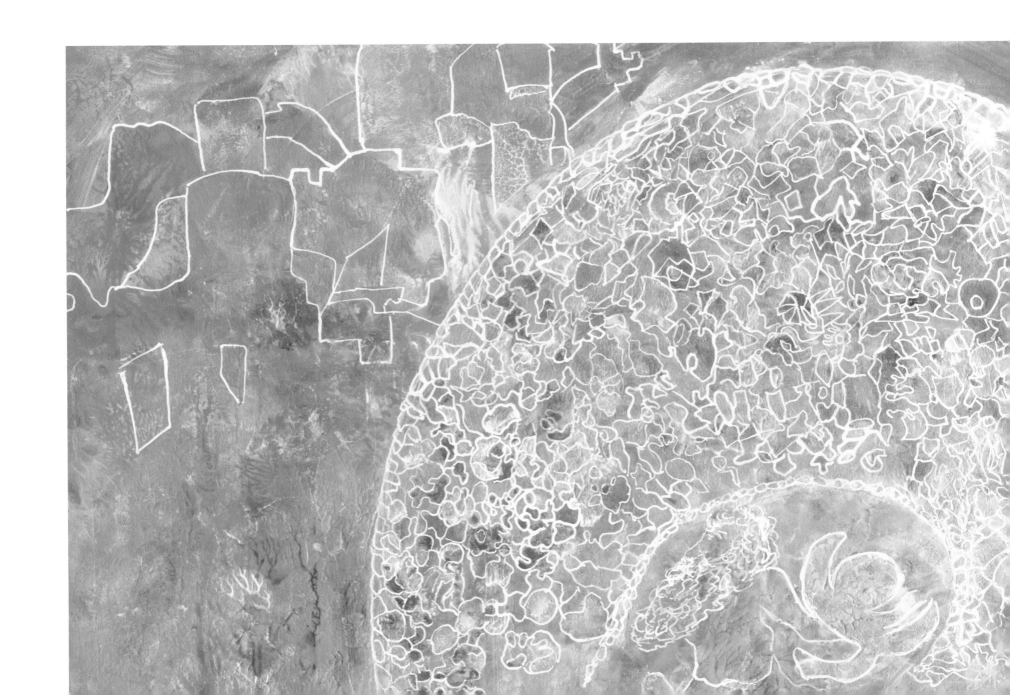

"No time to play," said Justgimious, even though he, too, was tempted to colorhop through the Kaleidoshop and view the variations in their wedged-edged,

and

tubular

transformations.

"How about a dreamsoda?" asked Spunktaneous. "A double-thick lunaberry shake at the Icedreamery?"

"No, Spunktaneous. Not before dinner."

Moths fluttered up, fluttered down, loopedabout in-and-out. "You're so busy," Spunktaneous told some moths who stirred a bowl of berrybatter.

"Busy? Us?" they said.

"Why, we never stop...

Baking and Making,

Shaping and Forming,

Turning out, Churning out,

Decorating, Adorning...

lunaberry ice cream, lunaberry cakes,

lunaberry pancakes and lunaberryshakes.

Lunaberry wafers, lunaberry chips,

lunaberry cookies and lunaberry dips.

Lunaberry hotdogs, lunaberry mustard,

lunaberry trifle and lunaberry custard.

Lunaberry burgers, lunaberry fries,

lunaberry toffees and lunaberry pies.

Lunaberry popsicles,

lunaberry jello,

lunaberry candy,

and lunaberry marshmallow.

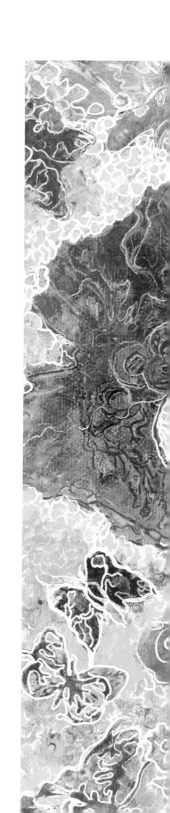

From mauve to pink to yellow to blue,

We stir, we sprinkle, we barbecue...

Then Justgimious and Spunktaneous passed

The Encyclopediary—

the repository for all Glimpsible information. This is where every Glimpsible learned...

exactly-and-matter-of-factly,

nine-hundred and ninety-nine of

JUSTGIMIOUS' ONE THOUSAND FACTS...

each fact, indelibly leaded by Fred—in sparkling red—into its cavernous foundations.

Next door, was

The Point -of- View.

From its multiangular balcony, Perceptilly taught her favorite subject:

Questions and Reflections.

"Every fact," she would say, "even one indelibly leaded-in-red—is open to scrutiny."

Justigmious then stopped at

THE NUSE.

"This, Spunktaneous, is the teashop where Glimpsibles muse while digesting the news—taking each word with a pinch—or sip—of Lunaberry Tea."

Justgimious and Spunktaneous continued down the street until they reached the Rotundary where the Glimpsible Sparks lived. Justgimious opened a red, wooden door: "Enter Spunktaneous."

Spunktaneous ran excitedly up the winding staircase leading to seven bubble-shaped rooms. "So **this** is what the Rotundary looks like inside!"

"An example of Gumptious' creative bubbulation," Justgimious informed Spunktaneous. "The six rooms, which are brightly colored, belong to the Glimpsible Sparks. They encircle a smaller one which will change to emerald green when the seventh Spark is chosen. The ceiling is high—useful for soaring. This is your room, Spunktaneous, for the next seven days."

"I wish I could live here forever," said Spunktaneous.

He jumped up and down excitedly, before springing up to the domed ceiling. "Imagine a round room in which I cannot be cornered!" he exclaimed, whizzing around without touching the walls. "And a round bed!"

Spunktaneous placed his sparkling jugglegems, which he always carried with him, underneath the pillow.

Farfetch,

Perceptilly,

Gumptious,

Gregarious

and Zippity

popped into his room to welcome him.

"Dinner is served, Spunktaneous," said Farfetch.

"Then, at blue o' clock, it's bedtime," said Justgimious, "and your apprenticeship with Farfetch begins when we wake up **precisely** on..."

the dot of turquoise.

A
Drooma
On the Take

The world of the Glimpsibles would have been perfect if it wasn't for the seven Drooma of Sooma Sooma, who had nothing better to do with their lackluster lives than eavesdrop on Glimpsibles...peep, peek, pry and snoop into the activities of their exuberant neighbors. They had no greater motivation, no grander aspiration than to steal and destroy everything in Glimpse, and no loftier proclamation than the one they had scribbled onto the door of their Grudgery:

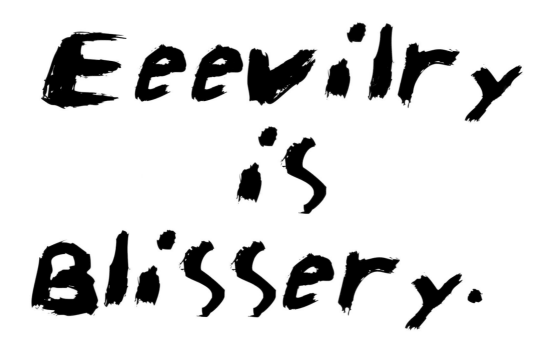

But the Drooma were almost evil; almost because they rarely could keep interested in anything longer than a split-grot—and being really evil took much longer than that. They called themselves **The Droops of Evil**, but, they were the worst Droops Evil ever had. They couldn't walk in a straight line, upright, with shoulders back and chests thrust out because they found it tiring. Nor did they know their right from their left, or their behind from their front. They couldn't march in procession, strut or swagger.

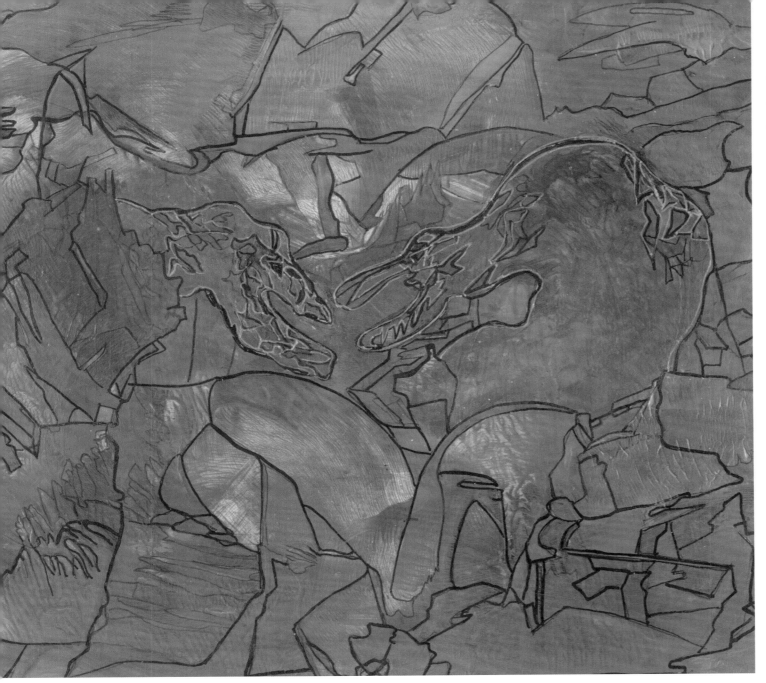

They could only droop, and they didn't do that well because they never drooped together. When one Drooma was drooping, another was walking upright. When one was walking upright, another was shuffling, slinking or lolloping. The Drooma never did anything together—but argue:

"You lost Justgimious' red!"

"No, you did."

"Yoooooou did!"

"You lost Farfetch's orange!"

"You did, and now you'll allow Spunktaneous to develop his greenessence! "

"NO, YOOOOOOOOU WILL!"

Squashed uncomfortably together in the Droomousine, their leader, Graball, at the faucet, their accusations overflowed as they argued all the way back to Sooma Sooma from the Droomasfear.

"We're hungry!"

"Nincomdroops! You just ate!" Graball was so angry that he crashed the Droomousine into the Grudgery. Soil, sludge, trash and corrugated sheets of roofing hurtled through the air, stunning a hoard of Clawhawks.

As usual, these scavenger birds were raiding the Drooma's plunderpiles.

"Out of the Droomousine, Droops!" Graball ordered. "March to Comocean! A plunge in that ocean will move you to motion—make you come up with a plan to exstrawdite Spunktaneous' green before he becomes a Spark. Forward March! Onwarddddsss!"

As the Droops trudged along the black and oily bogbeaches of Comocean, they passed mountains of junk, mounds of trash, hills of garbage and heaps of refuse.

Sooma Sooma was the junk dump of Infinity. Whatever was discarded from anywhere,

whatever was

dismantled,

deleted,

eradicated,

expunged...

could be found in Sooma Sooma: the worst of everything... and the worst of ideas.

The Drooma forgot to think of a plan as they marched, and as

the
Waves of Murk
came

CRASHING

all over them.

Although it was high tide, not even a bad idea surfaced.

"How refreshing," said Greasepot, diving through the crashbanging wreckage which hurtled through the waves.

Romping between rejects, kicking and splashing, they continued to scuffle and argue until Graball announced:

"Back to the Grudgery! Backward march!"

"Exhausting!"

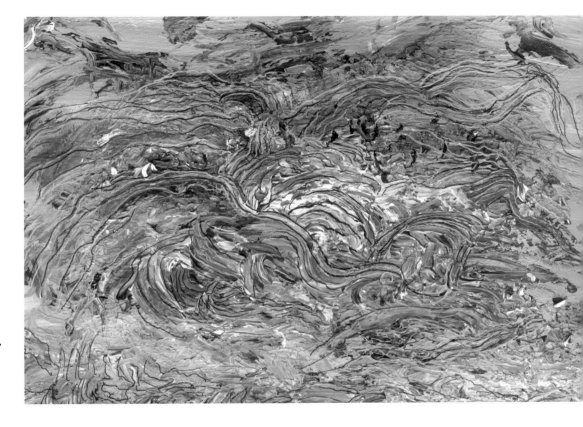

Once more, the Droops of Evil drooped...this time backwards...right, left, left, left, right, right, right, left, right, left, left, left, around, under, on top of and over each other. In lumpy, bumpy out-of-step steps,

Graball, the leader,

followed by Gungy,

Grotty,

Greasepot,

Grunch,

Grouse and

Grud,

drooped all the way to the Grudgery in the black hills of Sooma Sooma where they swooned into a deep slumber.

And while they slept, their ravenous snorerumbles dislodged dustdumps from the ceiling, batroaches from their beams, and shattered chandeliers onto their droopled forms. Even though outside the Grudgery, mountains of trash lunged into piles of stash, they didn't wake up until Graball did...with an idea:

"We'll do a Mockery!" he roared, kicking each of his Droops to attention.

"That's it—a Mockery," mumbled Grunch, struggling to sit up.

"Into the Droomousine immediately! There's no time to waste. We'll plot on the way to Glimpse..."

"But Graball, we need to eat," said Grunch, Grotty, Greaspot, Gungy, Grouse and Grud.

"GETTTT UPPPPPPPPPPP!" Graball roared. "You'll find trashburgers in the Droomousine for later—**when** you've plotted a plot. Do you want Spunktaneous to become a Spark before we exstrawdite his green?"

"We're so hungry!" said Greasepot.

"INTO THE DROOMOUSINE!"

Sighing, resignedly, their stomachs roaring with hunger, the Droops of Evil climbed once again into their vehicle.

"I'll steer," said Graball. "Grotty, let out the clutcher!"

But Grotty was too tired to lift his left leg. "It's stuck!" said Grotty. "Won't move."

"Then rev the diddler!" said Graball.

"Won't rev," said Grotty, his right leg dangling on the diddle.

"Won't rev? Must I do everything? Greasepot—you let out the clutcher and rev the diddler. Put your foot on the shaker and soup-up the swoosher."

"They won't budge," said Greasepot, slumping on his side. "Stuck."

"Bad timing," said Graball. "What a day to break down. Try the celebrator, Grud."

"Won't celebrate," said Grud.

"Enough drivel! Stop the dripe!" Graball commanded. "Now, one, two, three and together—

let out the clutcher,
rev the diddler,
shake the shaker and
swoosh the swoosher -

kick the diddly thing till it celebrates...now!"

"But we haven't had a chance to eat," Grotty complained.

"Nowwwwwwwwwwwwwwwww!!!!!"

As Graball's roars exploded through the Droomousine, and new cracks appeared on the walls and on the peephole in the ceiling, the Droops **revvvvvved** the vehicle up into the Droomasfear.

"That's it!" shouted Graball. "Together now, one-two-**THREEEEEE**..."

IN OUR DROOMOUSINE WE ZOOM.
WE'RE THE DREADED DROOMA.
WE'LL TAKE WHATEVER AND WHOM
BACK TO SOOMA SOOMA.

"LOUDER!" SHOUTED GRABALL

WE HAVE NO TASTE,
WE HAVE NO STYLE,
ATROCIOUS MANNERS, PREDATORY GUILE.
WE WANT IT ALL
EVEN IF IT'S FAKE,

A HAPPY DROOMA IS A DROOMA ON THE TAKE!

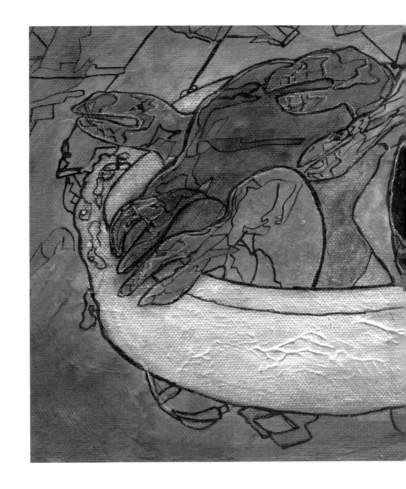

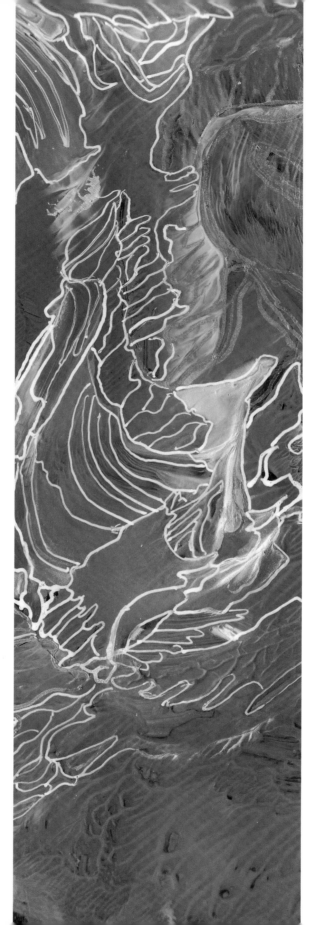

Nasal
Navigation

A nose wound around the entrance to Spunktaneous' room and sneezed loudly.

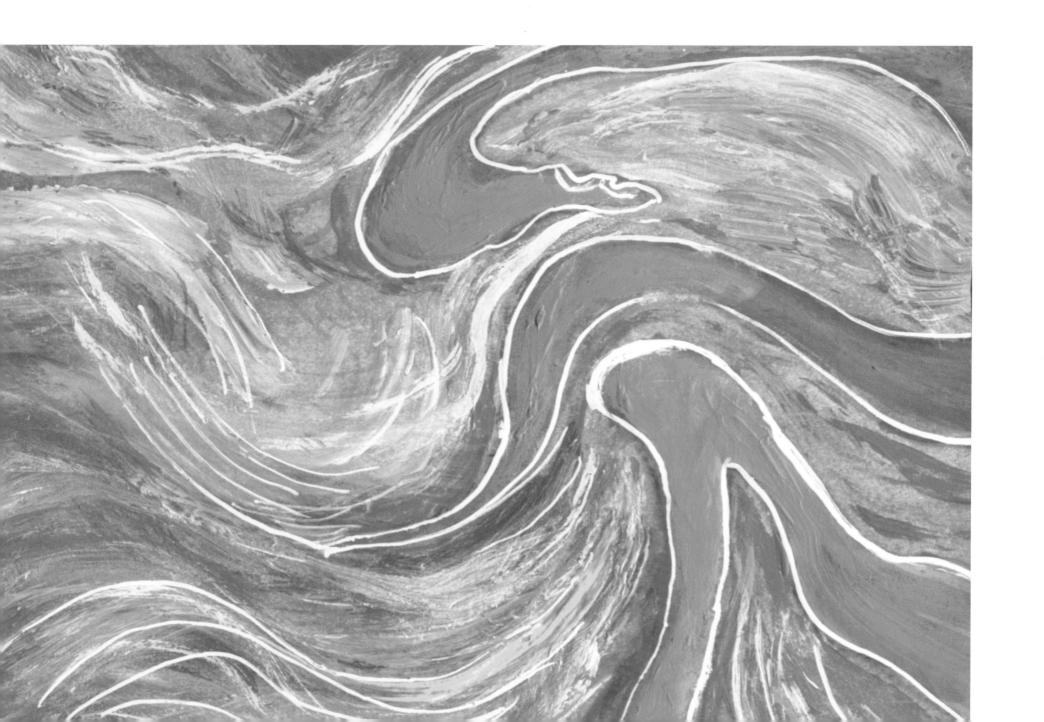

Spunktaneous sat giroof-upright in bed. "What is going on!" It was his first morning in the Rotundary.

"Your apprenticeship has begun, Spunktaneous."

The luminous, orange, undulating projection lurched forward and tickled him under his chin. "Out-of-bed! Out-of-bed! Dot of turquoise! Time to wake up!" Then, it hastily retracted, disappearing completely from view, before a startled Spunktaneous finished saying:

"Whhhhhoooooossssssnose!!!!????"

"Good morning. It's mine," said Farfetch a shadesec later, sitting on the edge of Spunktaneous' bed. "It's somewhat hyperactive today. But with my nose-shows, anything goes...anything neonoptic, anything concoctic, anything crackpotic...anything goes with my shnnnnowwwwws."

"But your nose is a normal size, Farfetch. That one was grots longer."

"Being a Spark is not easy, Spunktaneous," said Farfetch. "I extend myself—physically and mentally. Stretch and farfetch all extremities when necessary."

"Stretch and farfetch?" Spunktaneous asked.

"Always aim high, but remember: height is not the measure of height. **Aim** is. So aim more. Soar more. Never be aimless. Nor more-or-less. Be more-than-before. Much more. You must become perfect at what you're good at."

"But I soar perfectly already," Spunktaneous interrupted. "Higher than anyone else."

"Perfunctory perfection...a deception, Spunktaneous. Do you practice relentlessly? Assiduously? Like me? Why, at any ungiven opportunity I...

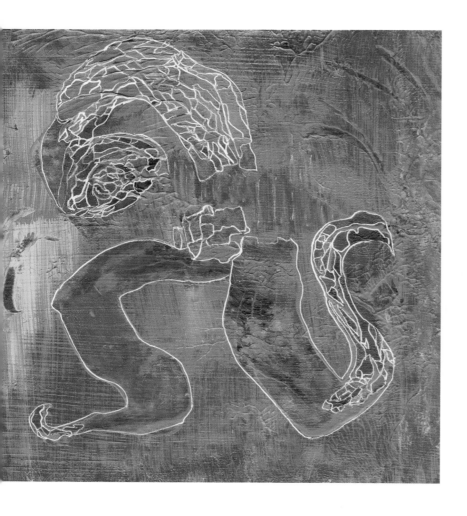

Practise my verse and impromptu rhymery,
Theatrix and slapbang one-linary,
Stretchlimbulate...an extennnnnnsive desiry,
I resulate on inimitable aspiry."

"But look at what I can do," implored Spunktaneous.

"No!" snapped Farfetch. "This is not only about you. If you are going to become a Spark, you first have to learn what the other Sparks do. That's what Justgimious has instructed." Farfetch held up Justgimious' instructions, indelibly written in red. "Listen carefully...

ROUTE TO SPARKHOOD—THE APPRENTICESHIP:

A candidate will spend one day with each Spark:

Day 1. Farfetch — Nasal Navigation

Day 2. Perceptilly — Perceptual Ilumination

Day 3. Zippity — Upward Perpendiculation

Day 4. Gumptious — Creative Bubbulation

Day 5. Gregarious — Headwhizzing Circumrotation

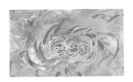

Day 6. VERSEBLURT CAFÉ — some revision and wordplay

Day 7. Justgimious—Essential Factulation—The Test.

"The **final** test?" asked Spunktaneous.

"Yes, in an absolutely matter-of-factly, then-and-there perfectionnaire, you will describe to Justgimious what each Spark does alone and together. If you answer all the questions correctly, and demonstrate your own ability to solve a problem better than any of the other candidates we've had so far, you will become the seventh and final SPARK OF GLIMPSE."

"Do I need to remember **everything**?"

"Everything—but, to make it easier for the candidates to recollect the information, we versify whenever possible—and, especially, at Verseblurt Café. What you need now is to understand our perfectabilities. Over the next few days, you will witness timing and perfection. See how Sparks do it alone and together. Quick, follow me outside because...

It's shnnnowwwtime!"

Farfetch rose rapidly into the turquoise sky. "Watch me, Spunktaneous!" He stretched his extremities leisurely...

first his toes,
then his fingers,
then his nose,

immmmmmmmmmmmmmmmmmmmmmmmmmmmmeasurably.

"Wowwwwweeeeeeee!" exclaimed Spunktaneous.

Farfetch flash-arced across the sky:

"Imagine...
Fingers which expand
and a luminous nose,
to follow wherever it goes...

"Imagine...

"Linguistic intelligence,
being rhymatically inclined,
with quickities abundant in a quixotic mind."

Farfetch's orange nose transformed into a lustrous, golden-amber illusionator. Then, dazzling copper, canary, and tangerine streamers streaked across the turquoise sky. They looped, zigzagged and volleyleapt into flashfluorestation as Farfetch danced through the arborial sky-splendour.

"Watch me

extremmmmmmmmulate my arms and legs,
somersault
from bough to bough with looooongulated, coiled fingers,

dizzyswing
in swirls of accelerating velocity...

round and round,
the Farrrrrrrrrrfetch-Go-Around."

Never before had Spunktaneous seen such strobefloodery—not even during dreamscendence.

"Come up here, Spunktaneous!" Farfetch called breathlessly.

Spunktaneous rose hastily into the sky and flashdashed through the Forest of Light until he reached Farfetch.

"Up or down?" Farfetch asked him breathlessly.

"Up and down," Spunktaneous replied, climbing up a translucent ladder forming in the sky.

They updowned the skyspringers, hopping from one diaphanous rung to another, until Farfetch commanded: "Now, follow me down!"

Spunktaneous hesitated because there were no downrungs in sight. They had melded into a smooth skidslippery of white. "I can't, Farfetch!"

"Just follow me! Do what I do! Glide!"

Spunktaneous hesitated, and then glided down the long lightshute after Farfetch. "Whatashowwww!" he exclaimed as he landed on his back on the soft grass next to Farfetch.

He looked up at the sky. The skystreamers had vanished, but, as always, a six-color rainbow stretched-arched over Glimpse.

The rainbow accompanied Spunktaneous back to the Rotundary, and appeared again that night in his deep, luminescent dream...

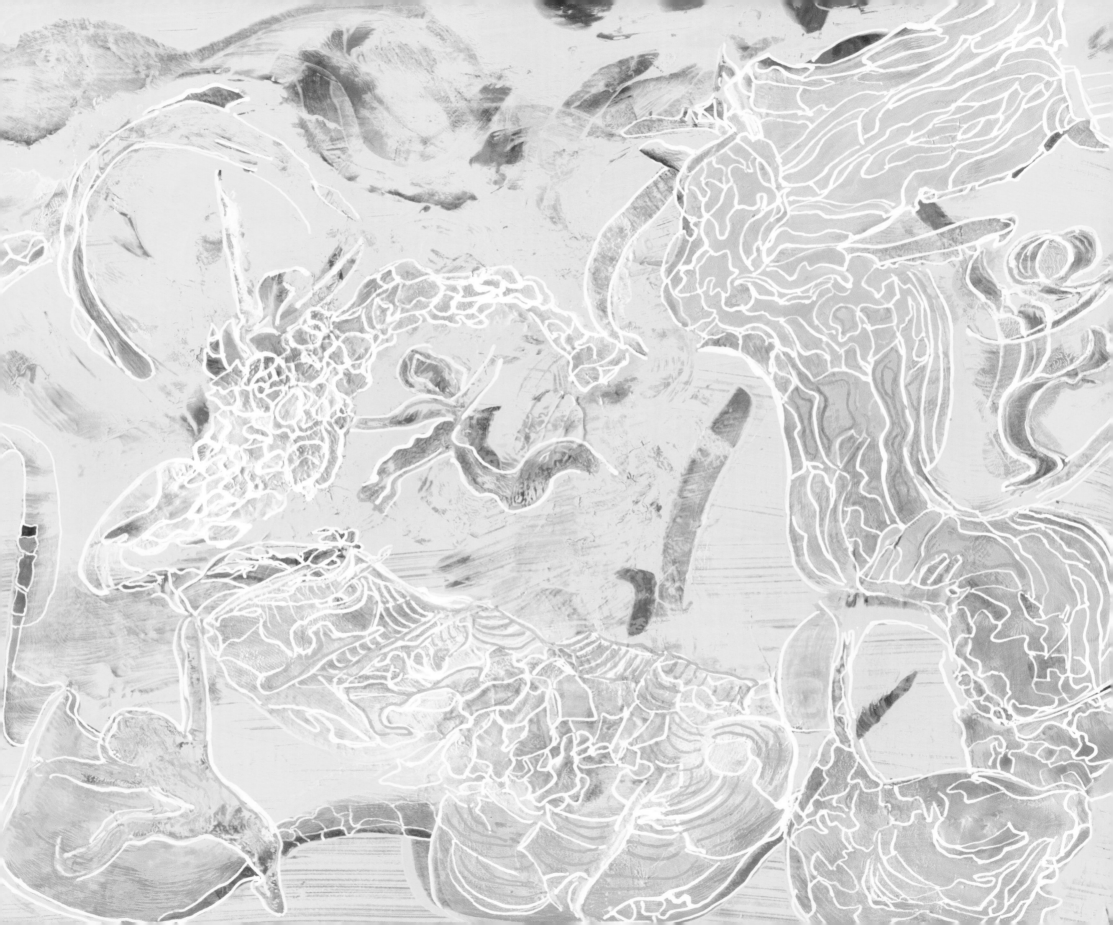

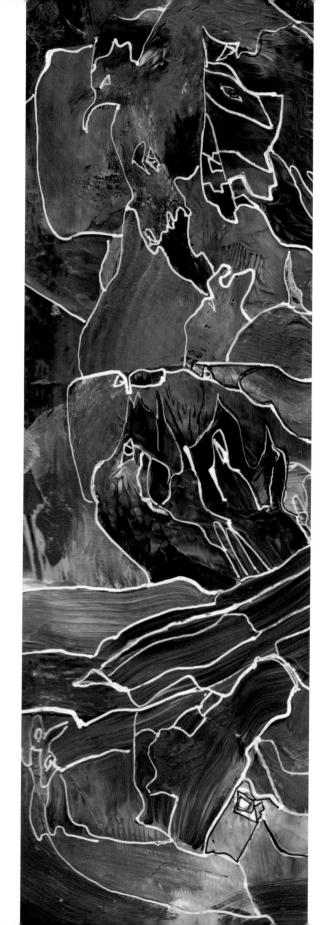

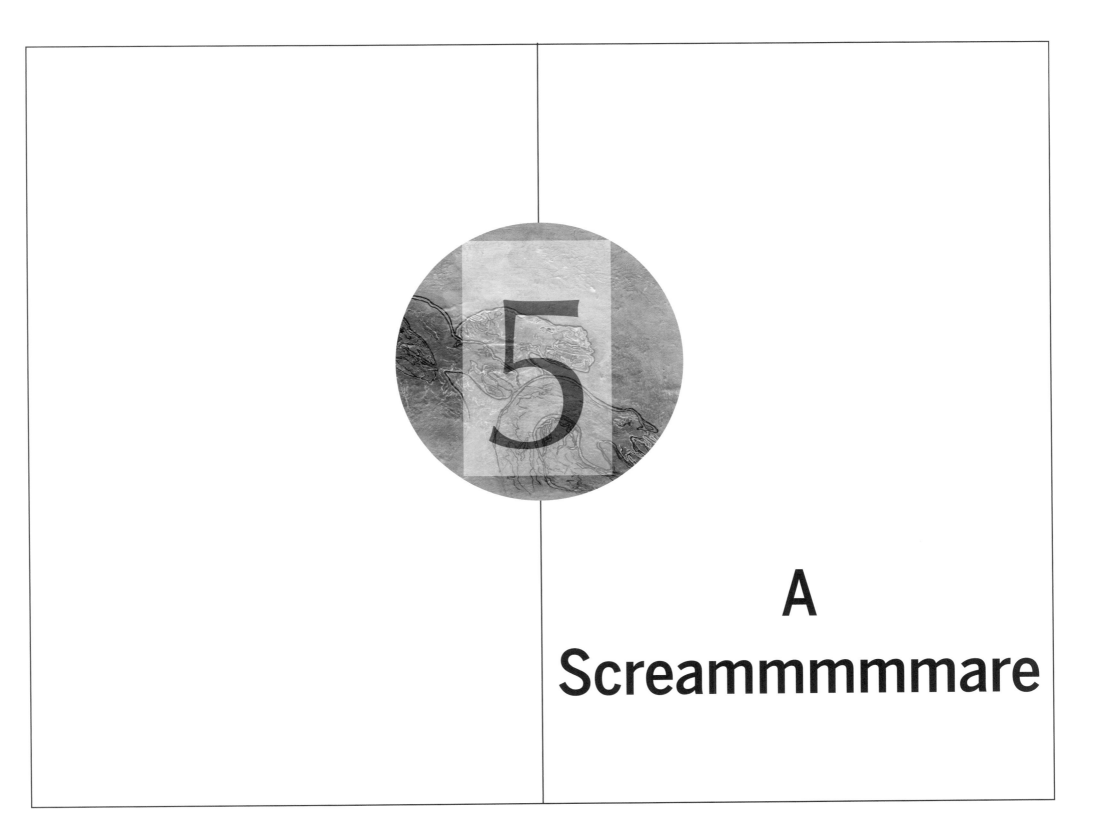

5

A
Screammmmmmare

That night, the Drooma entered Spunktaneous' dream:

"Oh, no!" he shouted.

The Drooma were chasing him! They wanted to kidnap him!

"Got you! I'm Graball, the leader."

"Let me go!" screamed Spunktaneous.

"My Droops have come to take you away," said Graball.

"To our somber..."

"Tasteless..."

"Litter-botched world of Sooma Sooma."

"We will drain you of your greenessence," said Graball.

"So **that's** why you are after me." Spunktaneous was terrified. "You want to kidnap me in case I become the seventh color of Glimpse's rainbow, and the source of its completion."

"Yes, and because," said Graball, "We simply are...

THE DREAM-CRASHING, DEBRIS-STASHING DROOMA OF SOOMA SOOMA,"

"Let me go!"

"No, **that** is not part of our plot! We'll never let you complete Glimpse's color-tight alliance."

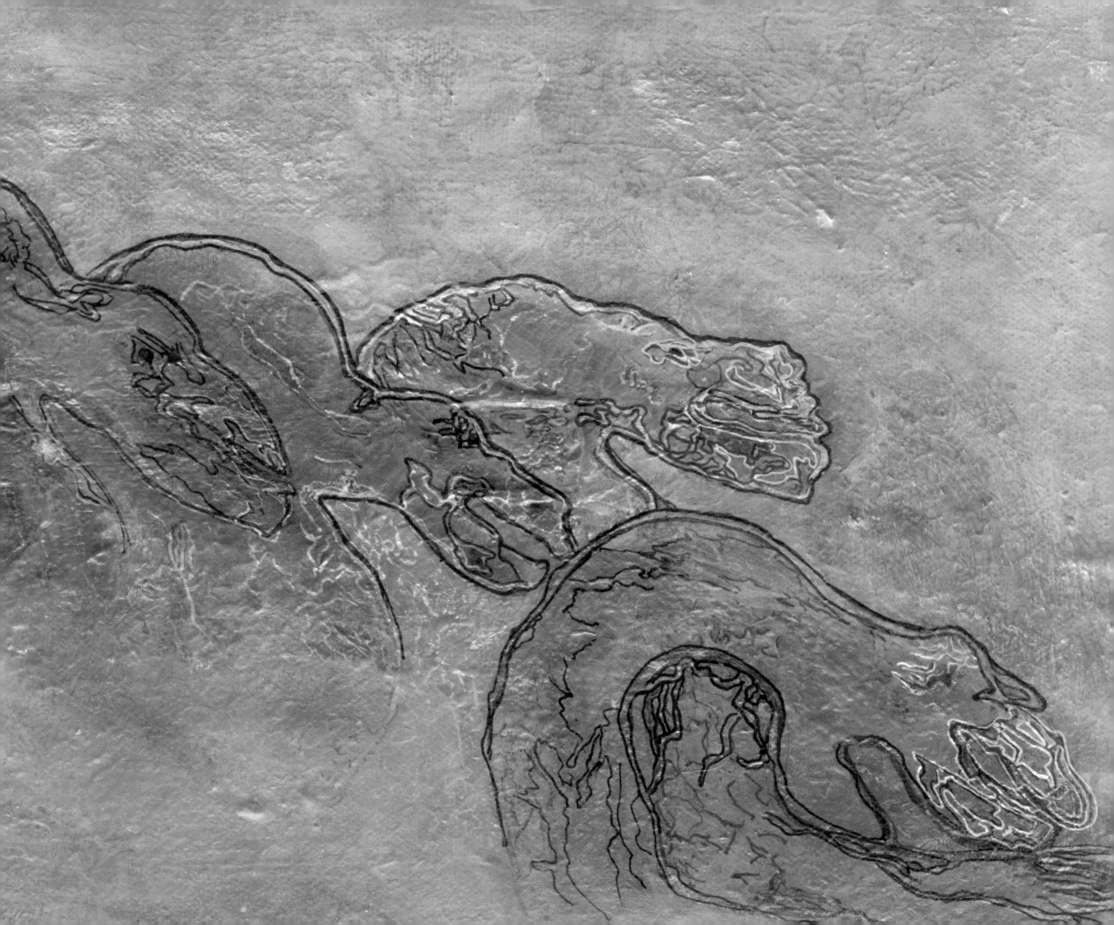

"But why not?"asked Spunktaneous.

"Because we want to continue to penetrate Glimpse—to plunder, destroy—eliminate all the joy of your world. Why should the Glimpsibles be happy if we're not? Besides, it's been hard enough dealing with a six-color alliance, but a seven color-tight alliance **cannot be allowed! Never!**"

"Why don't you create your own world of color?" Spunktaneous asked.

"Too much work. No time. Plotting plots takes up all our attention. Anyway, we want what you have—even if we don't need it. And right now, Spunktaneous, we want you to give our lackluster world a color-candescence, and your green will do—Spunktaneous-green—any hue,"

"So you want my color, even though you don't need it?"

"YES, GREED IS OUR CREED,"

said Graball. "Besides, we're tired of our murky monochrome. Let me formally introduce Gungy, Grotty, Greasepot, Grunch, Grouse and Grud. Let them each shake your hand."

"No!" Spunktaneous shrank from their extended thwackers.

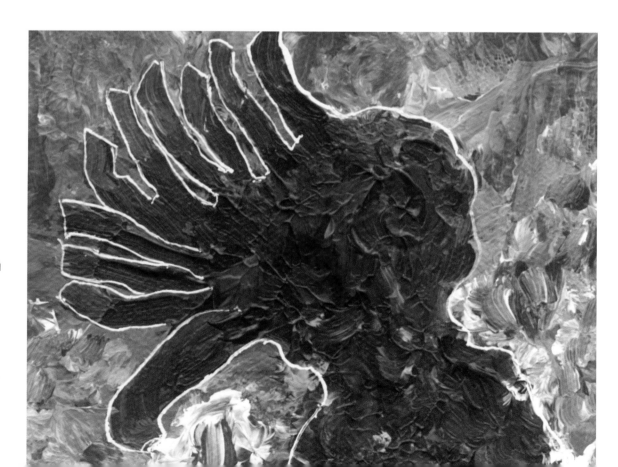

The Drooma glared avariciously at Spunktaneous. "We want, want...

WANT!"

Then the faces of the Drooma

as they recalled how, on previous occasions, they had failed to drain the glow from the other six Glimpsibles selected to become Sparks. With each new Spark, their penetration of Glimpse had become increasingly difficult.

"**This** time, we **won't** fail!"

"Through Exstrawsion, Spunktaneous, we will slurp up your green..."

"My greenicity—never! Color suckers," said Spunktaneous. "That's all you are. Spectroscopic parasites! Color your world yourselves! I'm not available. Goodbye!"

Spunktaneous twisted his body and loosened himself from Graball's waning grip.

"You'll never get away from us!" The Drooma lurched forward, pursing and protracting their dredgerlips into cylindrical strawslurps:

ATTACK NOW!
SNATCH HIM!
SNITCH HIM!
GRAB HIM!
GRASP HIM!
DREDGE HIM!
STRAIN AND DRAIN HIM!

EXSTRAWWWWWWDITE HIM!

"Let's plunge Spunktaneous headfirst into Comocean—with its clangorous, deafening debris! Quickly—let's catch him!"

The Drooma chased Spunktaneous through the dreary droomascape of Sooma Sooma, and what he saw there....

the sombre charred stubble-grass,

the gray smudgeweeds,

the smoky, grizzled Hills of Obsolescence, and

all the Drooma's

techno-illogical

botchery

saddened him so much that his glowessence began to fade...

glot,

by glot...

by quite a lot.

Spunktaneous was trapped in the pallid hopelessness of the Droomian world, completely surrounded by adversaries. He had no glow-power, no willpower, no will-to-go power.

"You're ours now." Graball prodded him hard in the ribs with his protracted strawslurp. "We have trapped you in Sooma Sooma. You'll never get away. Start climbing Mount Mockery—**now**!" he commanded.

"Mount Mockery?" Spunktaneous couldn't stop shaking.

Just then, a giant
rock formed in front of
Spunktaneous.

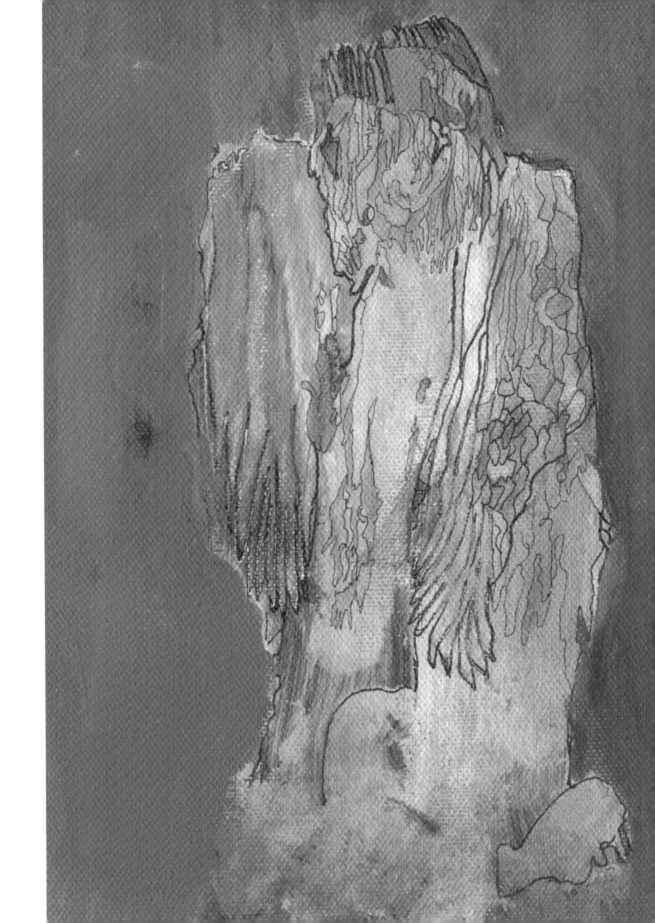

"Follow the Order of Appearance!" ordered Graball.

As Spunktaneous stepped onto the first rock, it rolled over and hurtled into Comocean, almost taking him with it. He quickly leapt onto the next rock that had suddenly appeared. It bulged menacingly in front of him, vying for his footing. Spunktaneous barely managed to leap onto the next rock, and the next one. Hastily, he leapt-stepped upwards along the steep incline, as emerging rock formations bullybashed the previous ones, sending them crashing downwards. Each new rock was fiercer than its predecessor, and each one looked even more angry.

Rock-faces of disdain, sneering and snarling, scoffed at his ascension:

"You're going to fall flat on your face, Spunktaneous."

"You have no courage."

"No abilities."

"We hate Glimpse. We hate Glimpsibles. We hate the Glimpsible Sparks. We hate you!

WE HATE!"

The slopes of Mount Mockery were vindictive, causing Spunktaneous to slip and stumble, but he never lost his grip. When he finally reached the summit, he was so exhausted that he could not move at all. His glow had faded glottonously. He felt doomed...gloomed.

"EXSTRAWSION!" shouted the Drooma.

Greasepot grabbed Spunktaneous and dangled him by one foot from the sheer cliffs of Mount Mockery. Terrified, Spunktaneous gazed down at raging Comocean so many grots below.

The Drooma taunted him: "How about a dip into Comocean, Spunktaneous?"

"A duck between the debris perhaps?"

While Greasepot jiggled Spunktaneous over the crashing waves of Comocean, the other Drooma formed a Line of Discordance along the serrated ledge of Mount Mockery. Then, lolloping their legs into the air and slapping one another with their thwackers, they blustered into song:

WHAT A SHAME,
WHAT A SHAME,
SPUNKTANEOUS IS DIDDERDANGLING IN OUR DROOMA GAME.

WELCOME TO SC-C-C-REEEEAMMARE
THE THOROUGHFARE OF DESPAIR
DROOPS OF GHASTLIES
EVERYWHERE!

WHAT A SHAME,
WHAT A SHAME,
YOU'LL NEVER ESCAPE OUR DROOMA GAME.

"Having a bad dream, Spunktaneous?" Greasepot threw Spunktaneous to Grotty...who threw him to Grunch...who threw him to Graball.

"He's mine!" Grud shouted, but Spunktaneous slipped through Grud's thwackers into the raging waters of Comocean.

"Help me! I can't stay afloat," Spunktaneous beseeched as cast-offs upon rejects crashed into him, reeling him in all directions.

Graball smirked victoriously: "You're ours now forever, so we'll linger along the ledge...watch you suffer."

Spunktaneous thrashed helplessly. He felt humiliated—soaked with shame. So scared—what's happening to me?

No forethought.

No morethought.

No simulthoughts in my head?

Are the Drooma winning?

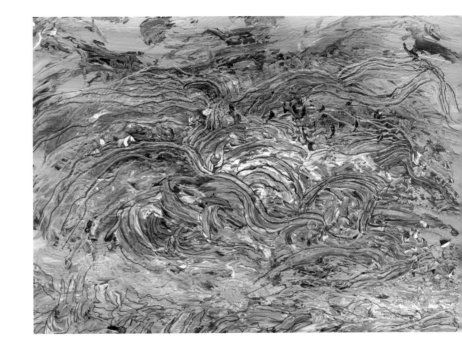

Spunktaneous heard Perceptilly's voice, but he could not see her:

 "No, the Drooma are **not** winning! Control your dreams! You can do it, Spunktaneous. You can push the Drooma out—far beyond the borders of your thought-quarters!"

"What are you doing in my dream?" Spunktaneous asked.

"Dreams have no doors," said Perceptilly.

Then Spunktaneous heard Justgimious and the other Glimpsible Sparks urge:

"Chase the Drooma away!"

"Rebuff them! Don't give them the attention they desire!"

"We're coming to get you, Spunktaneous!

YOU'RE OURS!

OURS!

OURS!"

Spunktaneous willed himself to ignore the threats of the Drooma. "Justgimious, Farfetch, Perceptilly, Zippity, Gregarious, Gumptious! I'll be back soon!" he shouted.

"Spunktaneous, you can leave Gloomland whenever you wish," said Gumptious. "There's nothing to fear." The Glimpsible Sparks had sleepsurged into a circumfluous dreampool:

"You can banish the Drooma, Spunktaneous," Justgimious urged. "Oust them!"

"Out!

Out!

Outttttttttt!"

spluttered Spunktaneous so loudly that he woke himself up from the depths of Comocean and caused the Drooma to dissipate into particles of frothy, foul air.

Still drenched from the waters of Comocean, Spunktaneous sat up in his bed wide-awake and exhilarated. The Sparks continued to sleep and snore. He wished they would wake up so that he could tell them that he had banished the Drooma. He had always felt safe before, knowing that the six Sparks would protect him and the whole of Glimpse from the dreaded Drooma. Perhaps, soon, he would do the protecting as well!

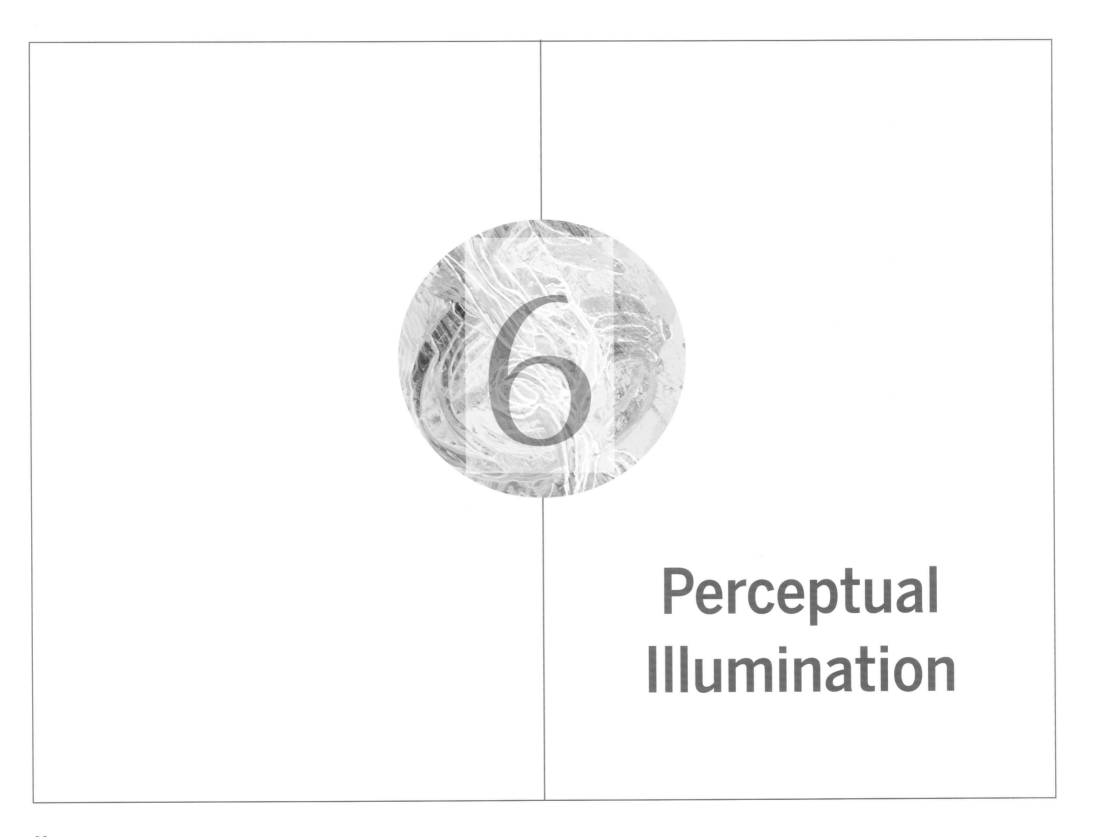

Perceptual Illumination

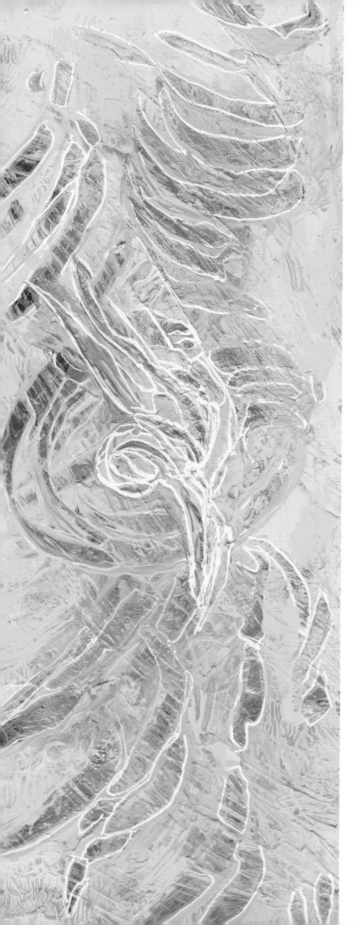

Perceptilly descended from the Any-Colored Sky. "Today's lesson is about **Color Perception**, Spunktaneous**.** Come, sit down and I'll teach you how to spot the exact point of a color change. You'll see that on the dot of noon, you'll be able to detect the ***Betwixt-and-Between***."

"Between what?"

"The Mid-Dot which separates morning from afternoon. You'll be able to see the skydot before it becomes a skyspot, and you'll recognize the slightest variation in a shadesec transfiguration—a very subtle change. It's important to be perceptive."

It was the second day of Spunktaneous' apprenticeship: Sunk-seated comfortably on a blue grassy mound, he wondered why Perceptilly had dropped so much deeper into hers than he had.

Perceptilly read his thoughts. "I'll give you a clue: The closer you get to reason, the more weight you have."

"Knowledge!" exclaimed Spunktaneous.

"Exactly," said Perceptilly.

Spunktaneous looked down majestically at her gold-amber hair. "Do I see gold as you do, Perceptilly?"

"Well, Spunktaneous....

I have a Master's Degree
In Meta-luster-cology.
I can glean a glitter from a glow.
Name all the lusters there are to know.

"But Spunktaneous, I don't know
how you see gold...or pink...or any hue.
Only you know. The colors you perceive
are entirely you, and each time you
look, they're different. Depends on your
moodprint which affects the glow you
give to a color."

Spunktaneous had a sudden urge to impress Perceptilly. He sprang up from the soft, grassy mound. "Watch how high I can go!" Then he crouched down low, and with arms outstretched and behind him, chin pointing upwards, he rose into the aquamarining sky...

spinnnnnnning,

spinning and turning,

soarrrrrrrrrrring upwards,

uuuuuuuuuuuuuuuuuuuppppppwards,

uuuuuuupppppppppppppppppwwwwwwwwwwwardssssssssss

perpendiculaaaaaaaaaaaarly...

until he reached the Lofty Lumisphere surrounding Glimpse. Never before had he reached such an elevation.

"Spunktaneous—you shouldn't be up there alone before you're able to recognize the slightest variation in a shadesec transfiguration, such as a Spot-of-Gloom—the warning that the Drooma are approaching."

But Spunktaneous was exhuberant. "What a view!"

From high up in the Lumisphere, Spunktaneous could see

the Wonders
of Glimpse

bathed in aquamarine:

the foaming,

fluctuwaving

Phantasea;

the Lake of Imaginings on which Glimpsibles floated and dreamed;

the Whooping Clock Tower which whooped with joy every time the hour changed. He could see

Lunaberry Forest,
where two million species

of vegivariation
intertwined,

and the scents

of one million
different flowers

mingled.

He could see the Dancing Fountains pirouette, and the melting, pink snow on Jumpaloon Mountains rivulet into strawberry swirlpools.

He could see the Skidslippery Pathways, so smooth and shiny that he glimpsed his own image reflected in them as he soared. "Perceptilly, I think I can see my green glow!" he shouted.

"Spunktaneous, come down! Hurrrrrrrry! Can't you see the Spot-of-Gloom above the Lumisphere?"

Spunktaneous chose not to listen to her warning. "Watch me spiral, Perceptilly—one thousand times without stopping at all!" He then vaulted and somersaulted over and over again until he was entirely out of breath. "Just a quick recess," he panted, "but don't go away—there's going to be much more today."

After sprawling, stretching, and orbiting on his back, round and round, and

up...up...uuuuuuuuuuuuupppppppppppppppppppppppppp,

Spunktaneous languidly opened his eyes again, and was startled by the truncated shadow of the Droomousine.

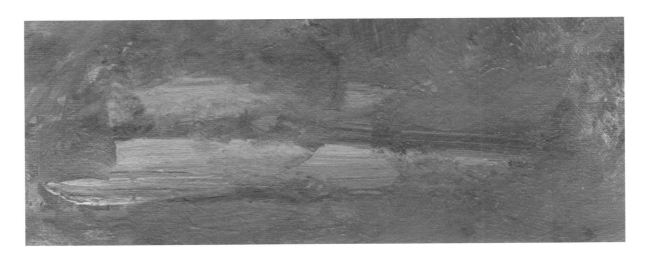

Terrified, Spunktaneous tried to change direction, but he could not. Instead, he was wrenched out of his depth, and hoisted upwards, wriggling and gasping, by the relentless pull of the Droomasfear...like a phantaphish on a line, coolly plucked from the Phantasea.

"Perceptillyyyyyyyyyyyyy! Get me down from here!"

Then shrieks and squawks shrilled in his ears and hot breath burnt his neck. Claws tugged on the hair of his head, and he was pulled into the litter-cramped, trashburger-jammed interior of the Droomousine by the Clawhawks of Sooma Sooma.

"Decided to join us, Spunktaneous? What bad luck. A hideous, hateful botchbungle," sneerleered Graball. "What a terrible pleasure! Into our domain you came—and, without an invitation."

"Let me go!"

"So awfully neighborly of you to pop into our Droomousine," rasped Greasepot.

"Nice of you not to look where you're going," scowled Grotty. "You didn't notice our Spot-of-Gloom?"

"Helllllllpppppppmeeeeeeeeeeeeeeee..."

"RRRRRRUGGGGGGGGGGGGGGGGGHHHHHHHHHHHHHHHHHHH!"

Spunktaneous' calls for help were submerged by a thunderous bellygrumble, followed by a dyspeptic urgle. The noise came from Graball who was overcome by hunger.

Like all Drooma, he had a never-to-be-satisfied appetite; but, unlike the others, he hadn't eaten anything ever since parading with his Droops in malformation along the Lumispherean border: a daily Droomanoeuvre...ever since spotting Spunktaneous and then waiting within the uncomfortable, trashburger-crammed interior of the Droomousine for him to orbit unsuspectingly towards the mangled vehicle...

with rusty faucets for steering,
a buckled bathtub-for-seating,
and a cracked peep-out in the ceiling
for squashing in,
squeezing out...
and spying on the Glimpsibles.

Graball had been so determined to capture Spunktaneous, that he had desisted the lure of the food on which his Droops had gormandized, despite watching them reduce a mountain of trashburgers to a meager stack—while the clawhawks devoured the remains and squawked for "morrrrrrrrrrrrrrrrsels!"

"No more!" Now, he **had** to eat. "The rest is for me!" Graball's stomach bellowed ravenously and ballooned into a quivering bulgebelly, trammeling Grotty, Gungy, Grouse, Grud, Greasepot and Grunch into the corner of the Droomousine. "The rest is for me!"

"Unfair! We can't budge," said Grotty.

"Cornered," said Grouse. "Mooooove your belly, Graball. I can't breathe."

"Got us at a disadvantage. That's not leadership," complained Greasepot. "That's despotic."

"Dispeptic," agreed the others. "Unjust."

"Got you trapped," Graball gloated. "You ate on patrol while I starved, so no more trashburgers for any of you. They're all mine!"

Nobody noticed Spunktaneous creep behind the stack of trashburgers. From his hideout, he watched in horror as Graball, smacking his semi-protracted slurplips, plunged voraciously into the burgers, diminishing crashing columns of Drooma inedibles into a tumbledown mound.

"Repelling," Spunktaneous moaned.

"Ooooofffffensive," roared Grud when he realized that Graball had eaten almost all the trashburgers. "Leave some for us!" Fisticuffing both of his thwackers, he thumped Graball in the abdomen. "Move your belly, Graball!"

"Happy to oblige. Hhhhhhaaaaaaaaaahhhhh!" Graball exhaled vigorously. "There!" Protruding his massive middle into a trouncing punchball, he catapulted Grud into Greasepot... Greasepot into Grunch...and Grunch into Grouse and Gungy...heads-first, locking them in an angry scrummage.

Graball gulped down more burgers. He grinned, his mouth trash-compacting. But he was running out of food, and Spunktaneous had to do something immediately before his hide-out was devoured. So, removing his jugglegems from his pocket, he leapt in front of Graball and

flashflicked

rubies,
sapphires,
and gleams-of-emerald
right in front of Graball's eyes...
dizzydazzling him into a deep
slumpdump.

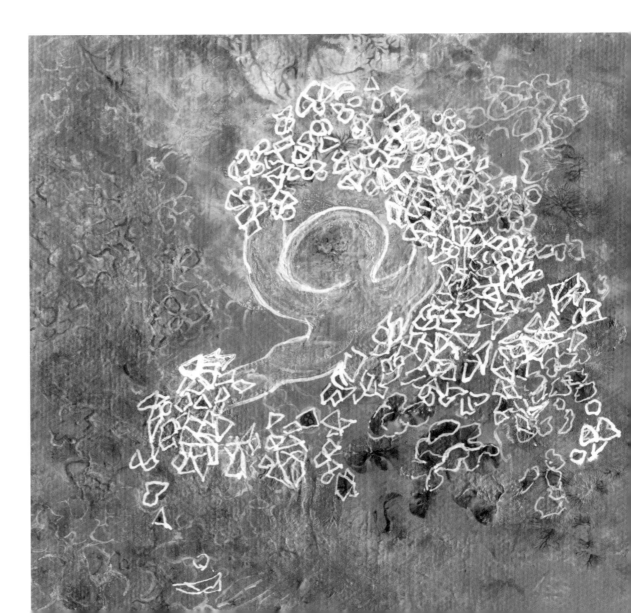

Snores exploded thunderously through Graball's slurper, swirling the air in the Droomousine into grimy circumvolutions which hurled Spunktaneous, coughing and spluttering, from one side of the vehicle to the other...and deflated Graball's belly, releasing his Droops from their corner.

Grotty tweaked Graball's nose. "Sound asleep," he confirmed, when Graball didn't stir.

"MUUUUUUUUUUUTINY!!!"

"We need new leadership. Why, we need someone just like me!" Greasepot, strutting up and down the Droomousine, beat insistently on his puffed-up chest with his clenched thwacker. "Just like me."

"NO, ME! MEEEE!"

And the Droops leapt onto Greasepot, squelching him to the floor.

Nobody remembered that Spunktaneous was in the Droomousine. They didn't see him edge towards the cracked peep-out in the ceiling, push it open, and begin to make his escape.

Cold, foul air gushed in, abruptly awakening Graball from his deep sleepslump to a view of Spunktaneous disappearing through the peep-out.

"He's getting away. Stop him!"

"We'll get you Spunktaneous! *OHOOOOOOOOOOOOOCH!*" shouted Grouse, Greasepot, Grunch, Gungy, Grud, and Grouch, colliding.

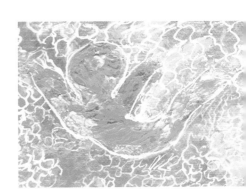

But before they could even pinch his shadow with their thwackers or slurp him up, Spunktaneous had disappeared into the thick gloom and haze of the clogged, criss-crossed shadows of the Droomasfear. He was overwhelmed by sadness. "If only I could feel a glimmer of brightness. I hate it here," he said.

He could see the Drooma burst through the peep-out and hear their taunts:

"You'll never get away, Spunktaneous!"

"You don't have a chance."

"We'll get you!"

"You're drifting towards us again, Spunktaneous," said Graball.

"You're doomed—there's nothing you can do."

Spunktaneous shut his eyes tightly, trying not to see the Drooma. He told himself: Transport yourself to Perceptilly. Don't get distracted. Thinklink into your coloressence!

He concentrated intensely. Streaks of hazy colors formed in front of him. They brightened, deepened...

into

streamers of yellow,

then ribbons of red,

orange,

blue,

indigo

and violet.

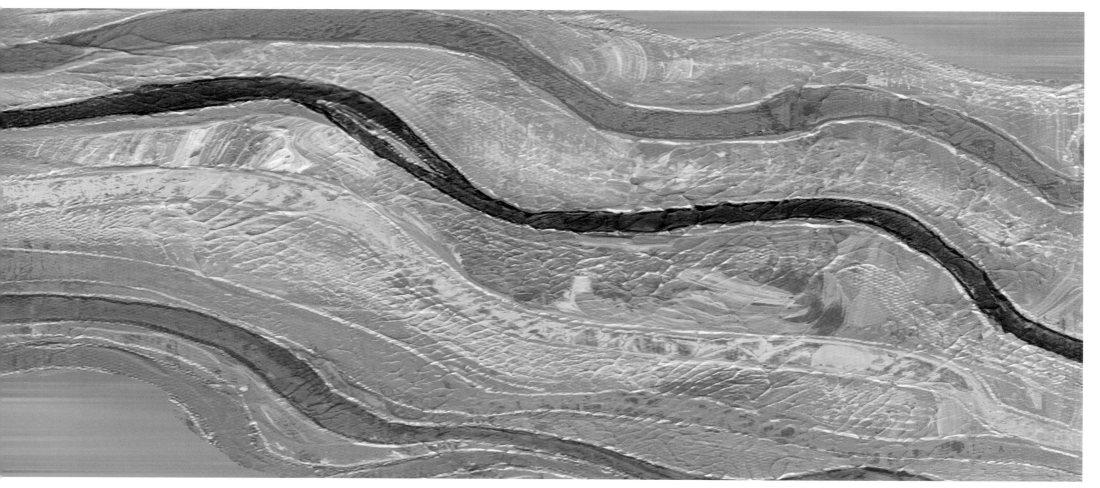

They waved at him, urgently beckoning him to follow.

"Perceptilly, Justgimious, Farfetch, Zippity, Gumptious, Gregarious!" he called. "I'm on my way back! I'll be there in a flash!"

When Spunktaneous looked back, he saw that the Drooma were close to him, but he also saw his own green glow—his greenessence. And so did the Drooma:

"Bottle his essence!" shouted Graball. "Snatch his green! Get him!" They scrambled to slurp him up.

"Helllllllllllllllllllllllppppppppp mmmmmmmeeeeeeeee!"

A green dot sparked in the gloom. It spread rapidly and thickened into a sheet of protection. A wall of olivine now separated Spunktaneous from the grasp of the Drooma!

"Oooooooh!" The Drooma slammed against the wall's cold smoothness. Banging on the inpenetrable enclosure barring them from the Lumisphere, they moaned:

"BUT WE WAAAAAAAAAANT SPUNKTANEOUS' GREEN!"

"I'm safe!" shouted Spunktaneous. "You can't get me!" And in a viridescent glow, Spunktaneous swooplooped back towards Glimpse...

just as the twinkblinking red skydot, separating morning and afternoon,

became...

a skyspot, blazing scarlet, crimson, and

ruby.

"Ohhhh wowwwwweeeee! *The Betwixt-and-Between!*

The Mid-Dot!"

As Spunktaneous flashed through the sky, he saw every gradation of the approach of the hour merge...

inwards,

outwards,

allwards...

until flaming red permeated the sky and his thoughts.

"I saw the Mid-Dot," he told Perceptilly when he saw her leaning anxiously over the marshmallow-soft mound on which he had landed. "and I discerned...

my greenessence!"

Welcome
to
Dilemma

"I'll show you how to do the *perfect* Perpendicular, Spunktaneous, with first an angular and then a linear velocity," Zippity said on Day Three. "The important thing is not only to make a speedy and lofty ascent, but also to return to the exact point of your departure. That's how you travel far while still remaining grounded. Watch me—and then we will do it together."

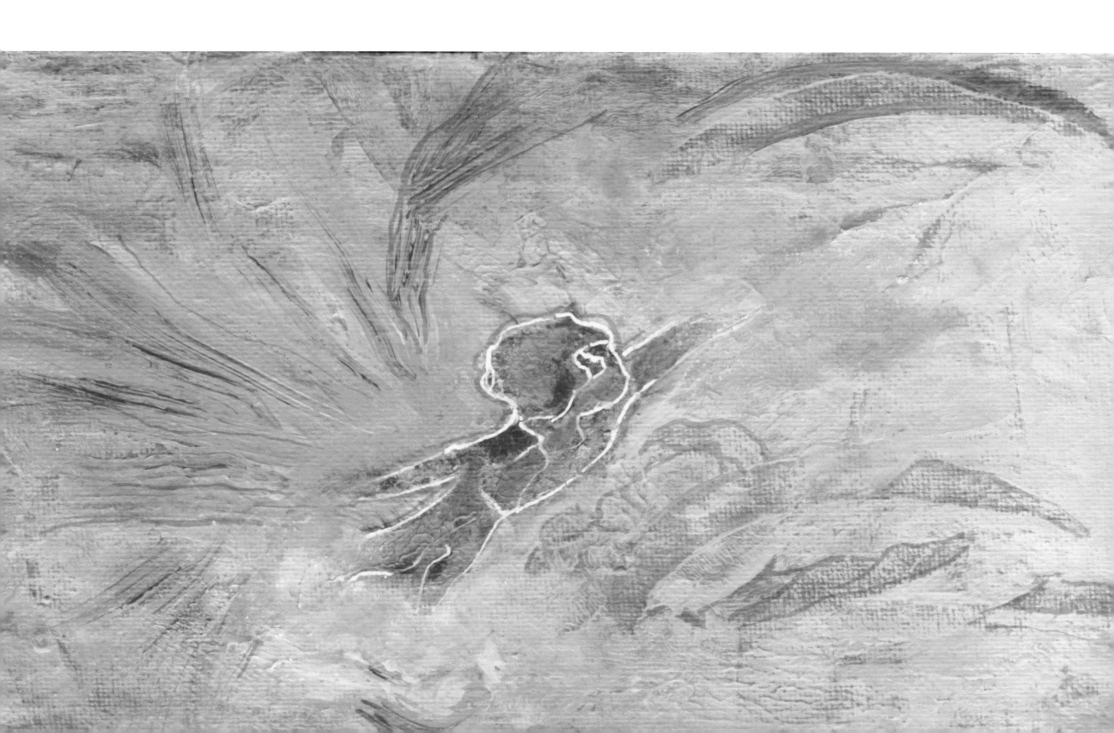

Even though Zippity and Spunktaneous had perpendiculared together all day, she hadn't allowed him to reach any grand heights in the Any-Colored Sky. "Now, this lesson is about doing the *perfect* Perpendicular. In case you haven't been listening to my instructions, I will show you again how to hold your body erect, taut, and streamlined, to ensure a vertical ascent—and safe descent. You should never rise before you are ready, and you should always adhere to the **Rules of Perpendicularity.** Watch me...

Watch me,

Zippity,

rise and reverse direction.

Watch me,

Zippity,

perpendicular with perfection.

I always practice protocol,

always am in control.

Neither a decision nor an intent

could be perceived as negligent."

"It doesn't look all that difficult," said Spunktaneous. "May I have my turn, now?" He didn't wait for Zippity to reply, but, instead, began to ascend vertically, rapidly…

Up, up,

Uuuupppp…

UUUUUUUUUUPPPPPPPPPPPP

with such careless abandon that he suddenly found himself, once again, in the Droomasfear.

"Being impulsive again, Spunktaneous? Can't keep away from us? Forgot to adhere to the Rules of Perpendicularity? What a welcome botchbungle. You're coming with us to Sooma Sooma. You'll not get away from us this time. You won't!"

"Won't!" jeered the other Drooma.

Their voices, appearing closer now, sent icy cold shudders through the Droomasfear and shivers up and down Spunktaneous' spine. Desperately, he tried to still his trembling body and make a safe desent, but he was being pulled further and further into the Droomasfear. He recoiled from the persistence of the rasping voices of the Drooma and the terror welling up inside him. "How do I get home? There has to be a way to return to the exact point of my departure!"

A glittering sign suddenly appeared in front of him:

WELCOME TO DILEMMA

Then more signs, beckoning gleaming messages, mottled into red, orange, yellow, blue, indigo, violet and green sparkle-flickers, each pointing in a different direction:

REDAWAY

INDIGO-AWAY

YELLOW-AND-AWAY

ORANGE-IS-THE-WAY

BLUE-WAY

VIOLET-WAY

THISWAY

THATWAY

ANYWAYYYYYYYYYYYYY

GREENWAY?

WHICHWAY?

The green sign flickered, but Spunktaneous didn't notice it.

The yellow sign glittered enticingly, pointing to a gleaming pathway of gold. "Must be the way home. I'll take it."

Spunktaneous proceeded along the pathway, enjoying the brightness of the route ahead:

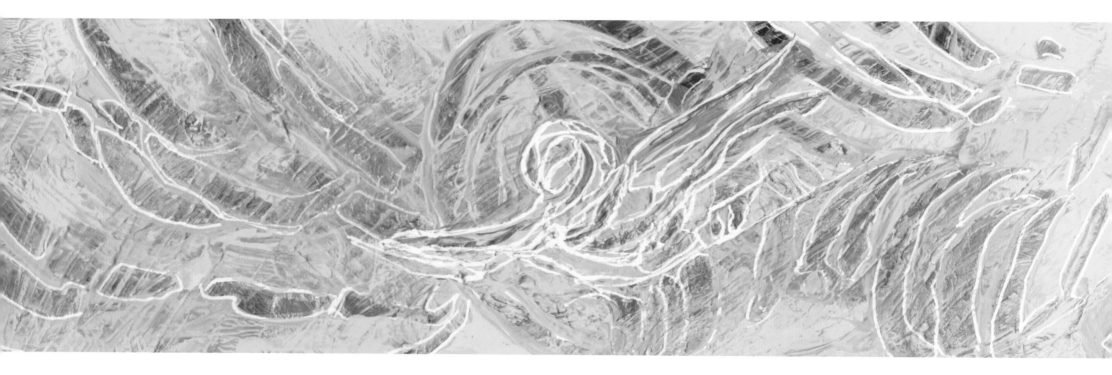

the shade-patterning
of arching evergolds,
and the flowering
goldelia
which grew along yellow
embankments.

He forgot about the menacing Drooma. As he bounce-walked on the quadruple-quick, he was constantly in the glow of a luminous figure gliding in front of him, illuminating the surrounding hillocks into glistening honeycomb mounds. "Please wait for me!" Spunktaneous called.

"This might help, Spunktaneous." The figure, turning to look at him for just a shadesec, extended beams of golden light to Spunktaneous.

"Perceptilly! It's you! And I'm on your pathway...it's not mine."

Immediately, Spunktaneous found himself back-sliding on an ebbing beam of light, retracing his steps to the beginning again...to the heart of Dilemma with its glittering signs. "Oh, which is my way home?"

"Think! Link to your color, Spunktaneous!" Perceptilly sounded far away.

This time, the flickering, green sign spun an emerald thread

towards Spunktaneous.

As he leapt to grasp it, he heard Graball roar:

"I see Spunktaneous! Let's grab him!"

Startled, Spunktaneous let go of the green thread. "Oh, which is my way home?"

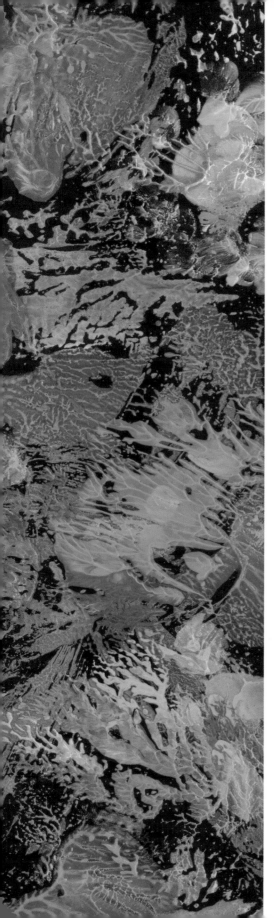

Again the glittering sign flickered bright red, orange, yellow, blue, indigo, violet and green, confusing Spunktaneous with their conflicting directions. "I wonder-whether...no time to wonder." And he leapt onto the radiant Orange Pathway beaming directly in his vision, leaving the angry sounds of the Drooma behind.

Spunktaneous meandered through

ginger marigold fields,

rambled up a glistening

marmalade sand dune...

and rolled down its slope

into an apricot sea

where a luminous, orange nose, snorkling to the surface, tickled him under his chin before plummeting again to the depths of the ocean bed and its colonies of copper coral. "Farfetch—it has to be you. This isn't my pathway!"

As soon as Spunktaneous acknowledged his error, he was backwashed to the marmalade shore...and bounced back to the heart of Dilemma, to the green sign urgently pointellating to the GREENWAY. Again he heard the Drooma call to him:

"NO! FOLLOW US TO SOOMA SOOMA!

YOUR PATH IS WITH THE DREADED DROOMA."

"Oh no, it's not!" Spunktaneous leapt onto the closest pathway...the INDI-GO-AWAY and was ricocheted to the surface of a huge, springy, souffleed bubble. "Wowwweeeee!" he shouted as he bounced up and down.

But the bubble began to deflate:

Phmmmmmmmmmmmmmmmm...

"Oh no!" Spunktaneous had pierced the domed surface with a jagged jugglegem which poked out of his pocket.

"Don't worry. I can repair it. You will see how I patch, gum-up, and reattach, when you spend a day with me— **Gumptious B.B.B.,** *the* **Best Bubble Blower**—an authority."

"Now I'm on your pathway. The wrong one, again. Right for you but not for me."

As soon as Spunktaneous realized his mistake, he was springboarded backwards to Dilemma, to the sounds of the Drooma smashing through tumbling rubble in the Droomasfear...to a green lightline fluttering in front of him...and to a brighter red line, which, rubying invitingly, beckoned to him. Spunktaneous made a hasty decision. "I'll take the red one."

As he bouncewalked along the REDAWAY which wound along the tall, burgundy brickstacks displaying indelibly leaded-in-red-facts, he heard Justgimious lecture him: "Concentrate, Spunktaneous, and no fiddle-faddle."

"Wrong again," Spunktaneous said, and he was thrust backwards to the beginning—to his dilemma, from where he chose to climb up Zippity's BLUEWAY. But, before he even reached the middle, he knew it wasn't his way.

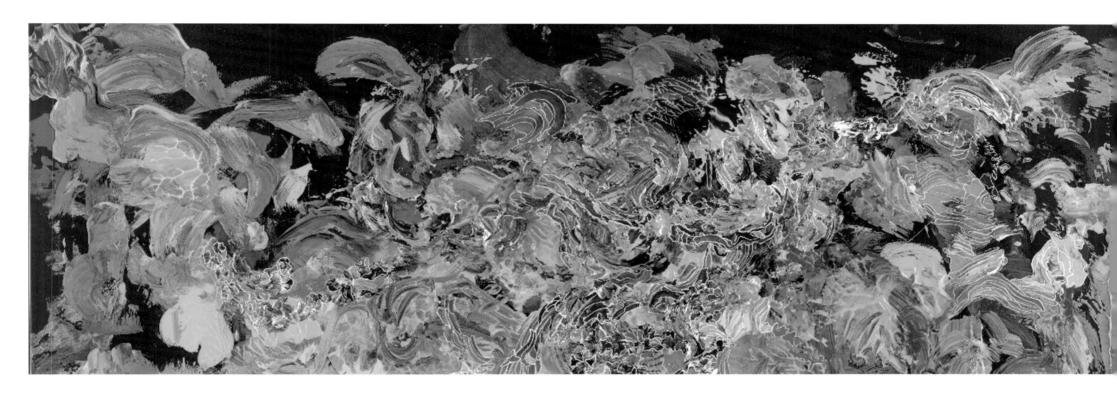

Nor was the VIOLET PATHWAY his way. He knew
it even before he heard a whispered instruction coming
from the longest of the rectangular flower beds, bordering
his route:

"Keep a tally, Spunktaneous, of every petalhead in every plantbed. I, Gregarious, with a circumrotating head, will teach you how to be punctilious."

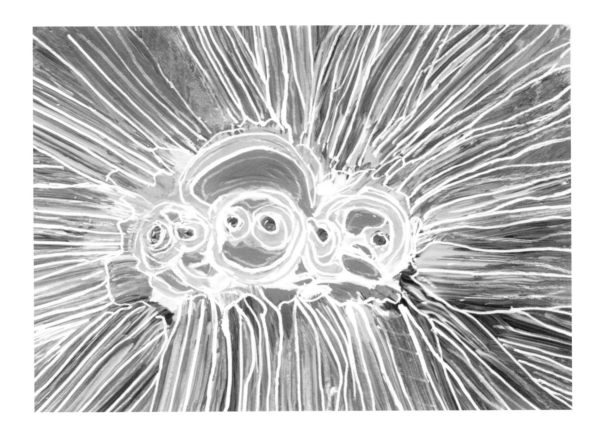

And Spunktaneous sprang off Gregarious' course...into Dilemma...and into the gloomy suction force of the Drooma.

"Got you, Spunktaneous! You still don't know your way?" Graball yanked him backwards into the Droomasfear.

"Let me go!" Spunktaneous shouted as he desperately stretched his body forwards, trying to reach the green lightline stretching towards him. But it receded from his view.

"No, that's not for you, Spunktaneous," said Graball. "You're coming with us."

Spunktaneous felt the hot breath of the clawhawks on his neck. "Oh, no! I won't go back to the Droomousine!" Thrusting himself forwards, he caught the tip of the thin thread at the end of the green beam of light, but, as he swung away from the clawhawks, they grabbed his feet, tugging him back into the Droomasfear.

"Let me go!" Spunktaneous held tightly onto the green lightline.

"You'll snap soon. Split in two," Greasepot warned. "You're stretched beyond your limits, Spunktaneous. We're taking you with us!"

"Never!" Spunktaneous clung with determination to the slender, green, flickering filament. "And I **know** my way home! It's the Greenway! It's my way!"

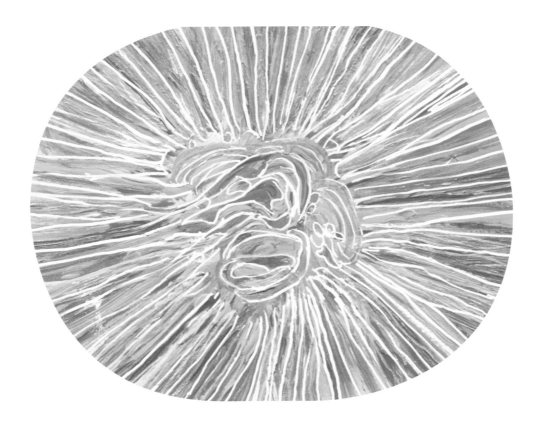

Immediately, the beam of light flashed bright emerald, and transformed into a skidslippery lightshute beaming perpendicularly all the way back to Glimpse, and to Zippity who had been waiting anxiously for him in the exact spot from which he had made his vertical ascent.

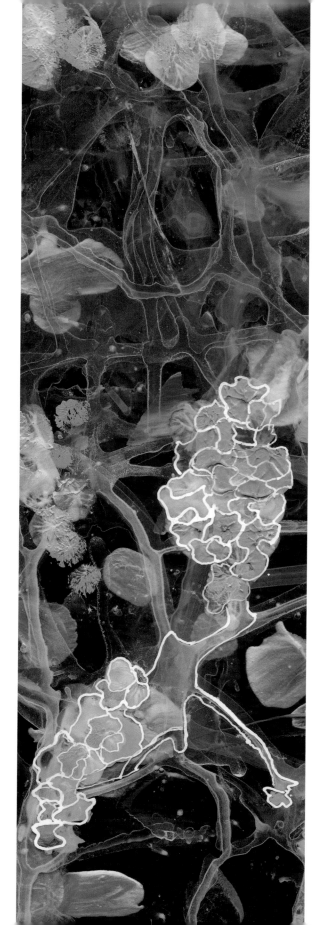

Creative
Bubbulation

"My turn to instruct you, Spunktaneous." Gumptious was seated at the curved foot of Spunktaneous' round bed. "Do you know why I'm called Gumptious, B.B.B.?"

Spunktaneous sprung out of bed: "No, why?"

"***Best Bubble Blower of Imaginary.*** I start with a tiny bubble of an idea, and then follow its unfolding potential. Each bubble is different. I never know what it will eventually look like. For example, I didn't know what your bed would look like when I started it. Neither did I know what your room, nor what the Rotundary would become."

"You didn't know?"

"No, I didn't. You see, I love the mystery of the unknown — and all its surprises.

"Do you know...

I can bubbulate anything!

I can create everything...

*I can create
bubble squares,
weighted and calibrated.
I can create
wedge-edge chairs,
innovatively created.*

*I can create
a bubble bed
designed entirely in my head.
I can create
lollipops—
for candy and bauble shops."*

"Do any of your bubbles ever not work out?"

"Do you mean, are any of them ever flops? Noooooooooooo! I can bubbulate anything! Everything! Come on a tour of Glimpse with me and I'll show you the variety of my bubbular creations."

Gumptious and Spunktaneous flew over the Rotundary, and over Lunaberry Street with its Moth boutiques.

They flew all over Glimpse.

"So many different shapes
and colors, Gumptious!

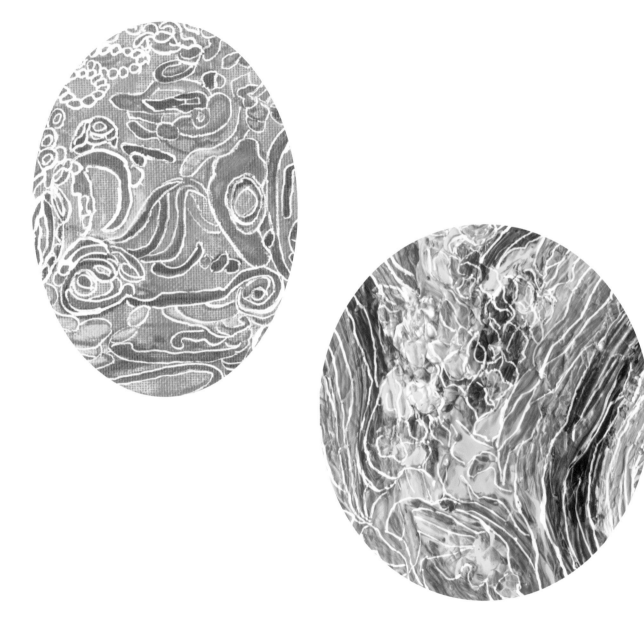

Wish I could make these."

"Come, have some fun with me in my bubble shop and I'll show you how I blow bubbles...

I create
nonstop
till I flop
and drop,
bubbles in my bubble shop.
Blobbular,
bubbular,
burbling bubbles...
from delicate singles to burgeoning doubles."

Spunktaneous watched in awe as Gumptious displayed his bubbular perfectability, and then, he, too, began to blow bubbles...one after another. "I love doing this!" he said.

"Yes," said Gumptious, "You understand that there are so many possibilities..."

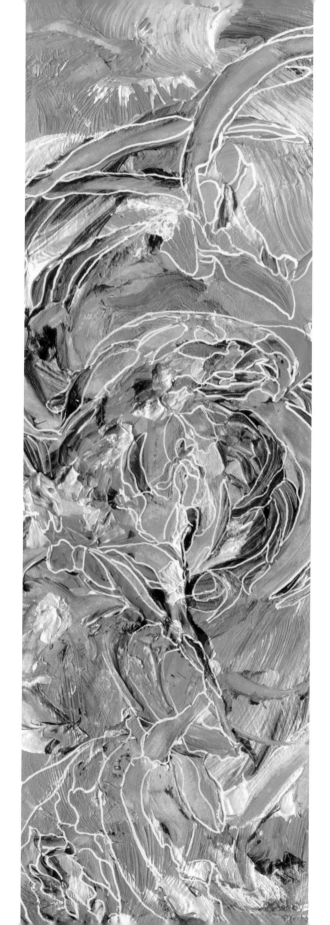

144

Punctillious
Itemization

"I really hope to be a Glimpsible Spark, Gregarious," Spunktaneous said on the fifth morning of his apprenticeship.

"Well, then you want to pass your test, don't you?" said Gregarious. "You need to learn all about my perfectabilities today:

computation,

categorization,

enumeration,

detailization,

and itemization."

"Let's begin. Firstly, why am I so well informed?"

"Is it because you are observant?"

"Yes, that's it! And it's because...

I have
a circumrotating head
which spins round
collecting information,
of my surroundings
in any location:
this location, that location...

this urban location,

that suburban location,

this recreational location,

that zoological location,

this insectile location,

that nautical location,

this equinoctial location,

that interstellar location,

this intergalactic location,

that infinnnnnnnnite location...

this location, that location, this location,

that location, this...that...this location...

that...this..."

I never forget...

Anything

I observe

Everything.

"Do you ever stop collecting information, Gregarious?"

"Never! Now yesterday, I counted one million and three purple petalheads in that flowerbed! You count them now, Spunktaneous, so that you can make sure I was **accurate**. Don't just accept what I say."

Spunktaneous felt quite dizzy after counting each petalhead, but pleased with himself that he had managed the task. "My tally agrees with yours, Gregarious."

"Good! You are learning about the importance of enumeration and verification. Come, Spunktaneous, let's fly over Glimpse together, and take note of its intricacies."

Gregarious' head whizzed round as he related the details of what he observed to Spunktaneous:

"Observe the fluted-florets with their slender cylindrical flowers which, incidently, make exquisite sounds in the wind. They are members of the Lunaberry Forest Orchestra. So are the windtrills—can you see them? They whirl in the wind while singing with crystal clarity. There is the Wandering-Rootabout, a nomadic plant that can root and uproot whenever it wishes. It's the resident dancer of the orchestra. Are you listening to the purple, snuffletrunk-ellipops truncate pop music? Did you know that their trunks also sniff in past, present, and future aromas of Glimpse simultaneously? Notice the very short legs of the giroofs—yet look at how long their necks are! See how they carry their babies in their backpacks when they hike. So many birds in Glimpse! They're part of the forest orchestra, too. Listen to the glow-quails, and merry-canaries. Can you hear the twoodle-aires

toooooooooootwoooooooodle, tooooooootwooooooodle.......

Toooooooooooootwoooooooooooooodle?"

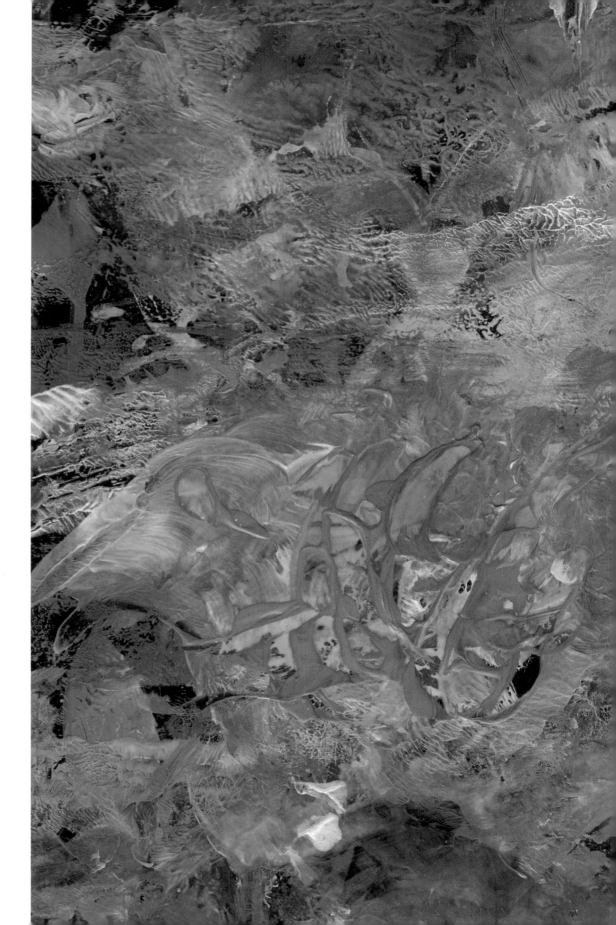

"Spunktaneous Are you listening?"

Spunktaneous woke up with a start. Never before had he fallen asleep while flying. "I can't keep awake, Gregarious. So much information."

"You've done well today, Spunktaneous. Always remember, details are important, especially if you wish to protect Glimpse from the Drooma. See you tomorrow at Verseblurt Café where we...

rhyme

to

remember."

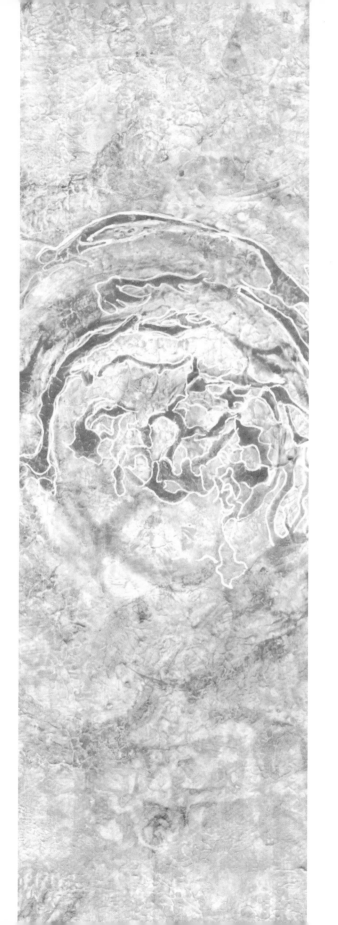

Verseblurt Cafe

Justgimious woke up very early on the sixth day of Spunktaneous' apprenticeship. He wanted to write in his Chronicles before joining the other Sparks at Verseblurt Café.

Comfortably sunk-seated on a marshmallow-soft, grassy mound beneath the Sagacity Bush, Justgimious chronicled the debut of Spring as it burst through the pink snow. He wrote incessantly, barely giving Fred an opportunity to veer off in new directions.

Even though it was cold and frosty, Justgimious continued to factulate amid the lunaberry bushes, the flip-flapping of frolicflies, and the lemon-fudge fragrance of emerging blossoms. Writing ceaselessly in **THE GLIMPSIBLE CHRONICLES**, he was unaware of the changing hues of the passing hours. Only when Fred, his lead chattering from the cold, refused, finally, to emerge from the snug, crumpled lining of Justgimious' jacket pocket, did he look up and see streaks of blue striating the golden sky. "What! Almost blue!"

Intent on reaching Verseblurt Café before the other Sparks noticed he'd been lost again in factulation, Justgimious raced down Lunaberry Street, at first oblivious to the fervent fussflappery of the Lunaberry Moths as they decorated the Flutterby Center with crimson banners and sapphire swirlstreamers, in preparation for the following day's test for Sparkhood.

"Should there be linear seating, Justgimious?" a Lunaberry Moth asked him.

Justgimious was forced to stop and give instructions. Breathlessly he said: "Yes, but there should also be a circular meeting of all the Sparks on the Illusory. Spunktaneous must face each Spark, so seat him on the swiveler."

When Justgimious burst open the front door of Verseblurt Cafe, Spunktaneous' review was already in progress.

"Were you lost in factualation again?" Farfetch asked Justgimious. "We've been versifying for some time, and you have interrupted me. As you know, Justgimious, **I'm** the resident poet of Glimpse, and for both reason and rhyme, I verseblurt all the time."

"Whether it works or not," said Justgimious.

"It always works!" snapped Farfetch. "I'm a natural at sound correspondence. A genius at verseblurt. Listen to my...

Syllabic recurrence
Vowel-consonant transference
Suffixal prefactmixtion
Triple-compound-fictiondiction.

Now you try:
Rhetorical ruminition
Rhopalical renderdition
Redundant repetition
Rhapsodic precognition..."

"What has all that got to do with Spunktaneous' test, Farfetch?" Justgimious felt exasperated by Farfetch's need to perform. "Must everything always be showtime? What about the lurking Drooma? I'm taking over now. Listen, Spunktaneous...

The Drooma are robbers, snatchers and thieves,
with many a diddle up their sleeves.
They scrounge, loot, nab, and rake,
hold-up, stick-up, and safe-break."

Gumptious interrupted: "My turn now...

They unlock secret combinations,
barge into cafes and versifications.
Con, snatch, snitch and slurp,
atrocious manners, they constantly burp...

Your turn now, Spunktaneous..."

Spunktaneous suddenly felt very anxious. "I really want to be a Spark," he said. "But I'm not sure I'll pass. There has been far too much information to absorb. Far too much...."

"Try to versify. It helps," said Perceptilly.

"All right," said Spunktaneous, "I will...

There's a whirlwind of words in my head.
Who said what and why?
There's whirlwind of words in my head
I cannot identify.

Did Farfetch say, 'Follow my nose?'
Did Justgimious say, 'That's a fact.'
Was it Gregarious or Perceptilly,
Gumptious or Zippity,
who got me so side-tracked?

There's a whirlwind of words in my head.
Who said what and why?
There's a whirlwind of words in my head
I cannot identify."

"Spunktaneous," said Perceptilly. "Why don't you sleeplink on it tonight, and tomorrow, when you wake up, you'll find you know **far** more than you think."

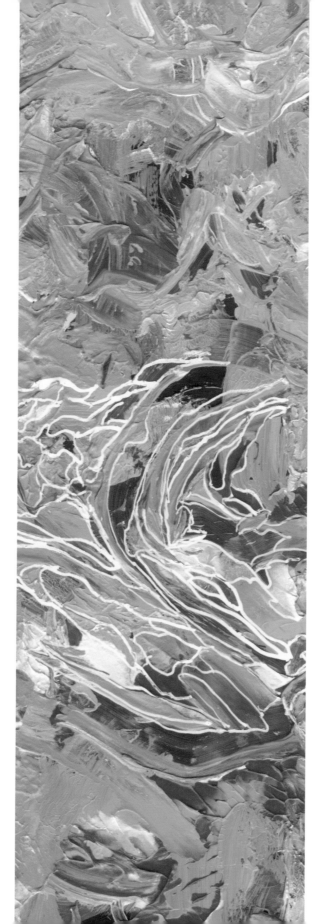

160

The Perfectionnaire

"It's time for your final test, Spunktaneous. Everybody's at the Flutterhigh Theater. Let's go!" Justgimious opened the front door of the Rotundary. "Oh look, Spunktaneous!"

A

red,

orange,

yellow,

blue,

indigo

and

violet

rainbow stretcharched from the front door of the Rotundary all the way to Flutterhigh Theater.

Justgimious and Spunktaneous ran beneath the rainbow's glistening arc to the theater where all the Glimpsibles of Glimpse had converged. They hoped that a seventh Spark would be chosen that evening, and, at last, they would be fully protected from the Drooma.

Perceptilly, Farfetch, Zippity, Gumptious, and Gregarious were already seated on the Illusory when Justgimious and Spunktaneous arrived.

"Sit here facing me and the other Sparks, Spunktaneous," Justgimious instructed. "The Perfectionnaire has three parts tailored to the particular candidate for Sparkhood. And it has a time limit. We will begin with **Individual Sparkhood**. Ready?"

"Ready." Spunktaneous' voice quivered.

"Spunktaneous, give me a summary in seventy shadesecs of what each Spark does."

Spunktaneous took a deep breath:

"Farfetch
extennnnuates extraordinarily.
Nasal navigation is
his sensolocation,
and he is also the Resident Poet of Glimpse.
He rhymes all the time."

"Well done, Spunktaneous!" said Farfetch.

"Perceptilly has a Master's Degree
in Meta-lustre-cology.
Knows a glitter from a glow...
all the lusters there are to know."

"I'm proud of you, Spunktaneous!" Perceptilly glowed golden-yellow, while the Phantasea rippled aquamarings of approval, and the giroofs unswivelled their necks erect-in-respect for his response.

"Good show, Spunktaneous!" The Glimpsibles of Glimpse whooped their support.

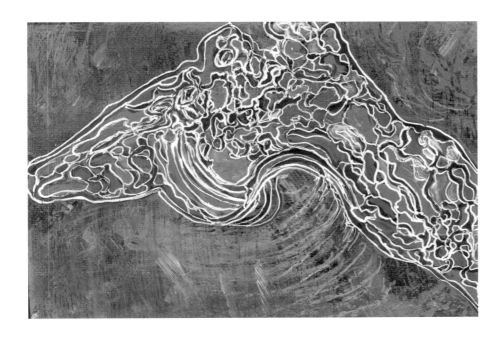

"Zippity is particular
about the perpendicular,"

Spunktaneous continued.

"Straight up into the sky she zooms,
in a continuous, unbroken,
vertical or angular line—
directly from her point of departure—
to which she always returns."

"Excellent, Spunktaneous," said Zippity.

"And Gumptious B.B.B., the Best Bubble Blower of Imaginary, creates architectural masterpieces.

"Gregarious has a rotating head spinning round collecting information of his surroundings in any location. He accounts for everything he sees.

"Justgimious factulates and allows no fiddle-faddle."

"Well done! Now for part two!" said Justgimious. "Describe in twenty shadesecs how Sparks form a color-tight alliance."

"Well, they can..."

Spunktaneous lost his concentration because he suddenly felt the presence of the Drooma and he heard them say:

"WRONG! HA! WRONNNNNNNGGGGGGG, SPUNKTANEOUS!"

"I'll repeat my question, Spunktaneous," said Justgimious. "Describe in twenty shadesecs how Sparks form a color-tight alliance."

"Thinklink, Spunktaneous or you'll run out of time!" Perceptilly urged.

Spunktaneous willed himself not to listen to the mocking voices of the Drooma which now had invaded his head: "**Together**, the Sparks form a color-tight alliance, and, by combining their individual perfectabilities, they protect Glimpse from the Drooma."

Justgimious pranced up and down the Illusory. "Well done, Spunktaneous! You have answered the first two parts of the Perfectionnaire perfectly— and with alacrity—but the third part requires a brief, thirty shadesec demonstration of what you can do when you're in a bind. So, invite a problem."

"Yes!" the audience urged. "A problem!"

"But why should a Perfectionnaire have a problem?" Spunktaneous asked.

"Because **everybody** encounters problems," replied Justgimious. "You have to be prepared for them. Are you ready to create and solve a problem, Spunktaneous?"

Spunktaneous, rose into the night sky, unsure of what to do. "All right, I'll start doing—something. I will juggle! Watch!"

Then Spunktaneous...

waved to the waving Phantasea,

skyrocked to the ellipops' roll on the ground,

and to the chimeroos' trounce-around the giroofs.

They all applauded jubilantly when Spunktaneous spun his sparkling jugglegems...with split-shadesec alacrity.

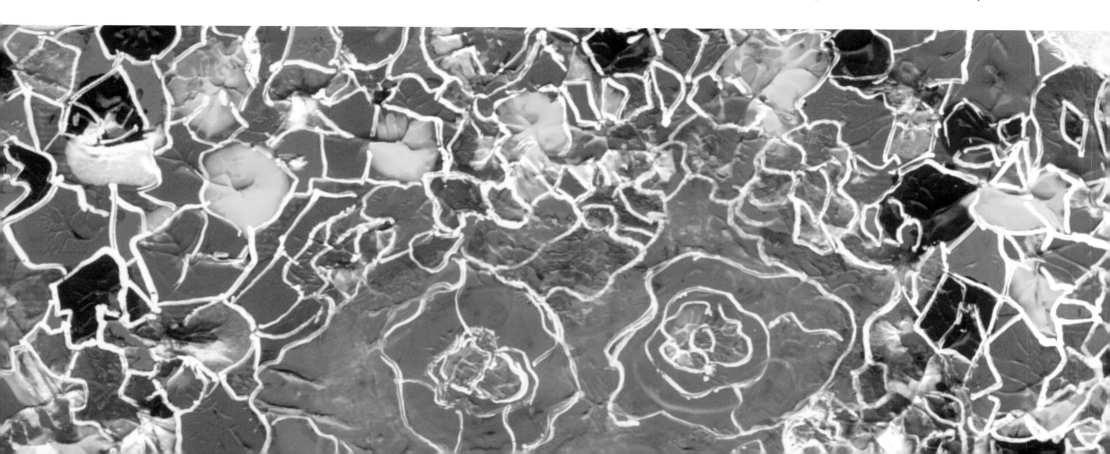

"Spunktaneous, you **need** a problem! You don't have time for fun. There's twenty-five shadesecs left. Twenty-four..." shouted Justgimious.

"I'm **creating** a problem, Justgimiiii..." Spunktaneous felt a strong tug behind him. He was being lifted up, up, upppp—beyond the Any-Colored Sky into the Droomasfear.

"You're running out of time, Spunktaneous. You're going to flounderrrrrr," taunted Graball.

"No color-tight alliance for Glimpse," said Gruesome.

"I'm not scared of you. I'm going to become the Seventh Sensoproblematic Interplanetary Spark. You'll never be able to penetrate Glimpse again!"

"No, you're not going to become the Seventh Spark because we're going to stage a Mockery and infiltrate any thought of it," said Graball.

"We're going to slurp up your green," said Gungy.

"No color-tight alliance for Glimpse!" shouted all the Drooma.

"Noooooooo! Watch!" Spunktaneous threw his jugglegems up into the

Droomasfear. They hurtled around him...

enlarging

ballooooooning

twistorting...

into shimmering, polychromatic particles, causing the Drooma to shield their eyes and recoil from their brilliant glow...but only for a moment.

The faces of each of the Drooma skewed grotesquely into seven, menacing, bulbous rock faces of...

DISDAIN

DERISION

SCORN

SCOFF

CONTEMPT

RIDICULE

AND CONDEMNATION.

171

"Help, Justgimious!"

"Don't allow them to infiltrate your mind, Spunktaneous! You can do it!" Justgimious watched helplessly from the Illusory. He could not interfere with Spunktaneous' test for Sparkhood. "Time is running out, Spunktaneous!"

"Perceptilly, help me!"

"Remember, only **you** can stop the Drooma, Spunktaneous. Don't acknowledge them. Don't give them credence!" said Perceptilly. She shut her eyes tightly, quite unable to watch Spunktaneous without intervening.

"Eighteen shadesecs left, Spunktaneous. You can do it!" urged Justgimious.

"But I don't know what to do!"

"Fifteen shadesecs left, Spunktaneous! You can still be a Spark," Justgimious urged.

"Fear creeping up on you?" Greasepot inquired contemptuously.

"So easy to crush you to quiv-v-v-v-erines and slurp up your greenessence," said Gungy disdainfully.

"Face it, Spunk," said Gungy. "You can never be a Spark."

"Thirteen shadesecs left!"

Spunktaneous was filled with despair. "I'm not going to be a Spark after all."

"Find a solution, Spunktaneous!" Justgimious shouted. "You have the ability! You have what it takes to be a Spark!"

Just then, Spunktaneous' attention was caught by a glittering signpost pointing in different directions:

REDAWAY...

INDI-GO-AWAY!

WHICHWAY?

ORANGEWAY?

"Having a dilemma, Spunk?" Graball scoffed.

"Nooooo! I'm not having a dilemma, Graball."

"Of course you are, said Gungy. "You're lost."

"No! Neither lost nor scared. You will not stop me from becoming a Spark! I know just what to do! I will follow **my** pathway—the **greenway**!"

"Just ten shadesecs left!" he heard Justgimious call.

Spunktaneous resolutely glared at his fears inside...one by one, until the rock faces of

DISDAIN

DERISION

SCORN

SCOFF

CONTEMPT

RIDICULE AND

CONDEMNATION

crumbled together into the Droomasfear.

"Just five shadesecs left!" shouted Justgimious.

The green sign sparkled brilliantly and in a flash, Spunktaneous jumped onto the GREENWAY. "I found my path! I'm on my way!"

In a viridescent glow, he swoooooooploooooooooped back to Glimpse.

As he flitted across the Lake of Imaginings and sailed across the Phantasea, he saw his glowing green reflection rippling in the water. "Just look at my glowessence!" he exclaimed.

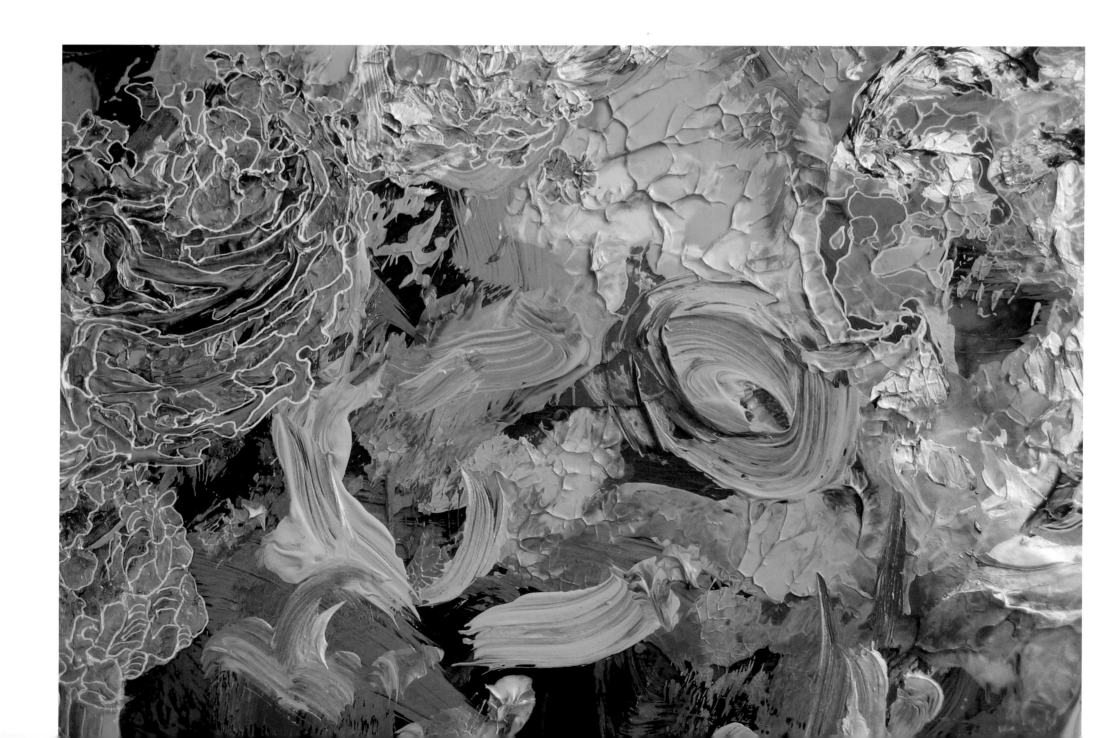

And the night-blue sky flashed

red,

orange,

yellow,

blue,

indigo,

violet...

and then...

green,

emeralding
all
of Glimpse.

Spunktaneous
landed on the
Illusory, on
the exact
point of
his departure.

"You are the Seventh Spark of Glimpse, Spunktaneous!" Justgimious was jubilant. "The search has ended! You've passed with flying colors! Your greenessence now completes our color-tight alliance."

Then

Justgimious,

Farfetch,

Perceptilly,

Zippity,

Gumptious,

Gregarious,

Spunktaneous...

and all the Glimpsibles of Glimpse rose into a many-colored sky, and sang:

We are the Glimpsibles, flying through the sky,
spinning, twirling, whizzing up high.
Looking at Glimpse from another point of view,
seeing things differently, doing what we do.

We are the Glimpsibles having so much fun,
flying in a pink-blue sky with a turquoise sun.
Looking at our world from way up high,
looking at Glimpse from an Any-Colored Sky.

Flat out we must race,
greased lightning right through space.
Flat out day and night
on a fantacosmic flight.

We zoom and zip,
rapt in awe, a wonder trip
to worlds far and near,
we zoom in top gear.

We are the Glimpsibles having so much fun,
flying in a pink-blue sky with a turquoise sun.
Looking at Glimpse from way up high,
looking at our world from an Any-Colored Sky.

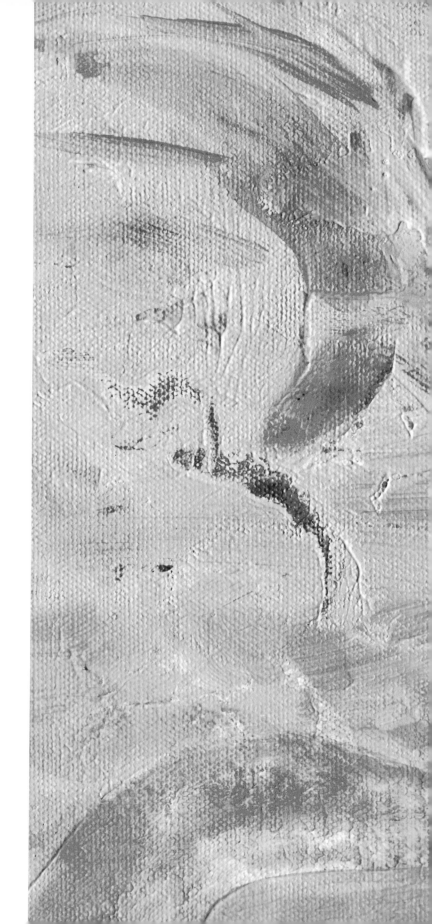

The truncated shadow of the hovering Droomousine is still visible, but now, the rainbow, which stretch-arches over Glimpse, has seven colors...

Justgimious-red,

Farfetch-orange,

Perceptilly-yellow,

Zippity-blue,

Gumptious-indigo,

Gregarious-violet and...

Spunktaneous-green.

Glimpse is secure, and, at midnight, Lunaberry Forest shines emerald.

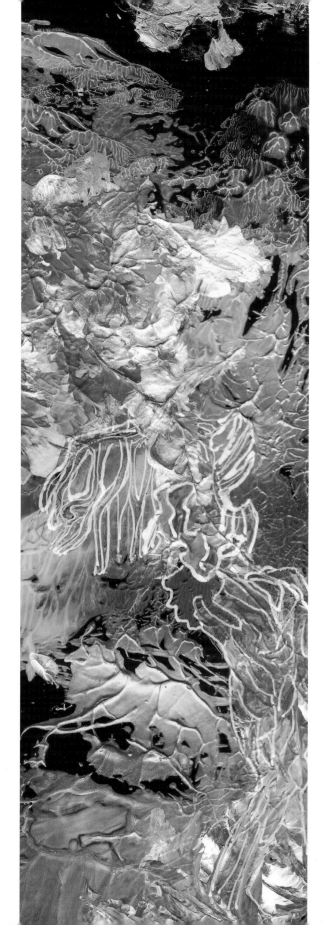

The
Never-End

The world in Justgimious' head continues to enthrall him. Notes, scribbles, doodles, reveries and imaginings fill his notebooks. He allows no interruptions when he writes, especially from Fred, who still contributes when Justgimious isn't looking.

Justgimious now lives permanently in the World of
Glimpse. He has followed Fred's advice:

Skedaddle

from your mind

all you know.

Some...

Fiddle-faddle

will unwind

your flow.

By...

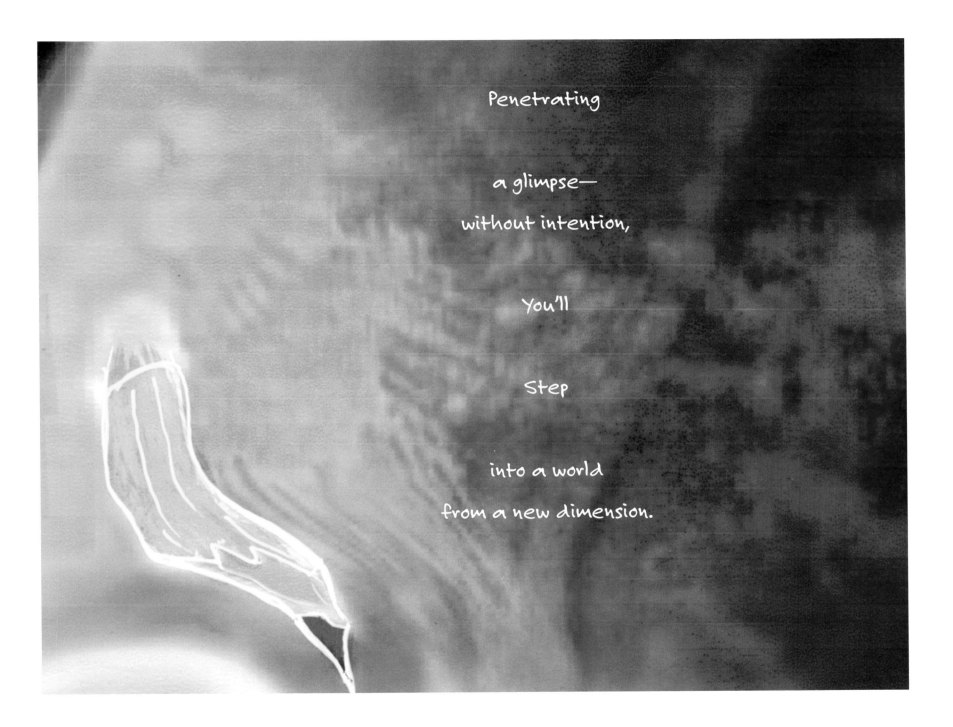

Penetrating

a glimpse—
without intention,

You'll

Step

into a world
from a new dimension.

189

If you...

shut

your eyes,
you'll hear

some cosmic verse...

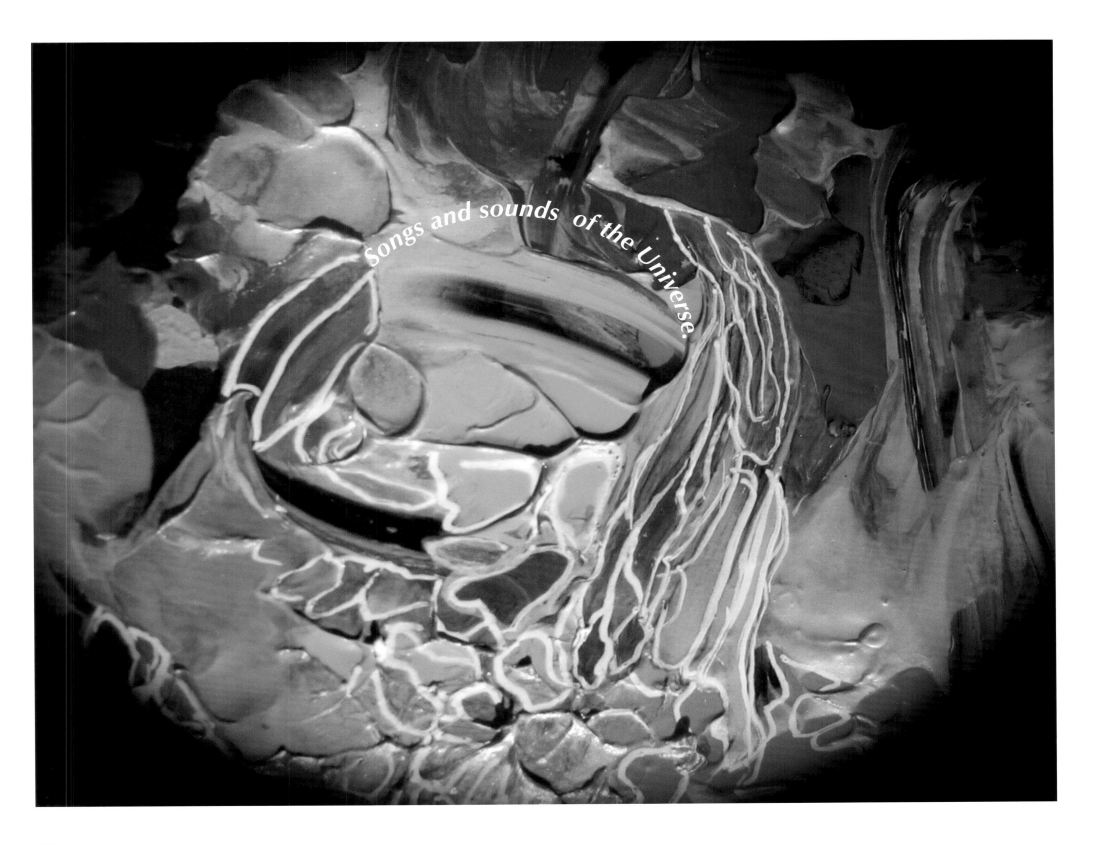

Songs and sounds of the Universe.

191

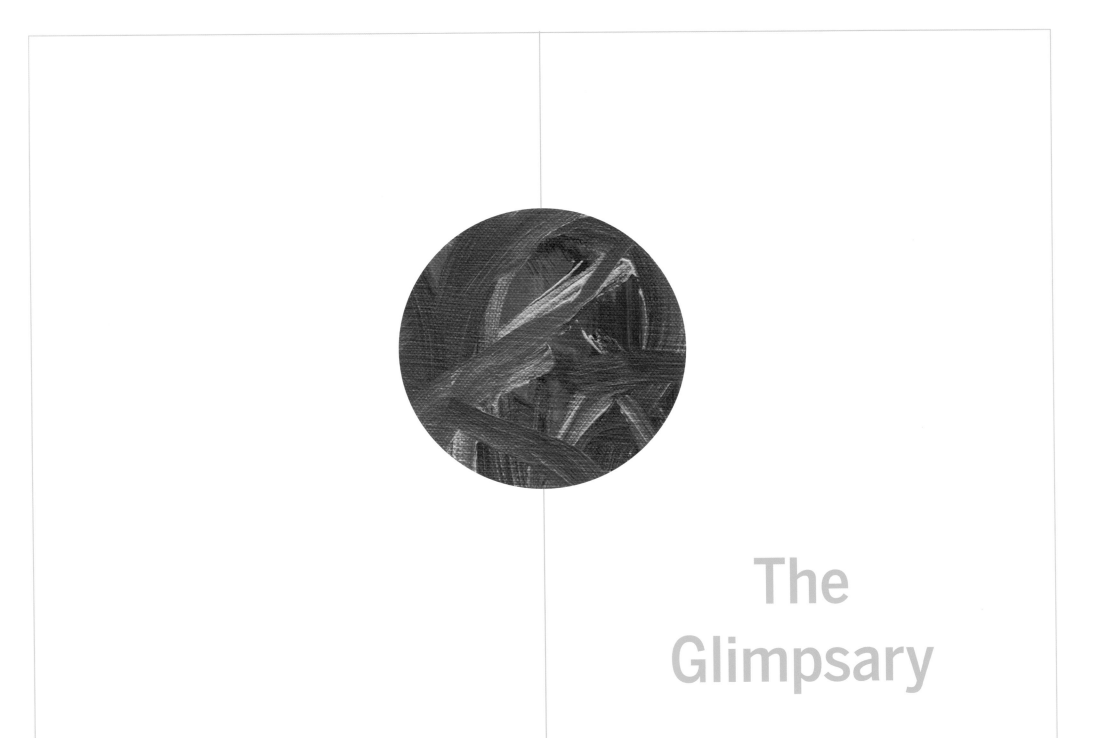

The
Glimpsary

Any-Colored Sky: in Glimpse, the sky changes color hourly during the day. At midnight—once Spunktaneous becomes a Glimpsible Spark—it will become emerald green.

Batroaches: cockroaches which are the size of bats and hang upside down.

Beforethought: a mode of Glimpsible thinking comparable to intuition.

Berrybatter: made from Lunaberries.

Betwixt-and-Between: the skydot before it becomes a skyspot.

Bogbeach: the oily, murky, polluted beach of Sooma Sooma, which runs along Comocean.

Bounce-walking: fastest when done on the quadruple-quick, with a rockwriggle-rollabout swingspring, it is quicker than walking or running, but not as fast as soaring.

Bubbular: the shape of Gumptious' bubbles.

Bubbulation (Creative): Gumptious' art and Perfectability. His bubble-art is aesthetically pleasing.

Glimpse: the world of the Glimpsibles, surrounded by the Lumisphere.

THE GLIMPSARIAN CLOCK—A.M. to P.M.

Glimpse	Earth
Turquoise (Dawn)	6a.m. -7a.m.
Aquamarine	7a.m. - 8a.m.
Azure/Lilac	8a.m. - 9a.m.
Violet	9a.m. - 10a.m.
Mauve/Purple	10a.m. - 11a.m.
Purple/mauve	11a.m. - 12 noon.
Mid-Dot	the separation of morning and afternoon
Red (lunchtime)	12 noon - 1p.m.
Pink	1p.m. - 2p.m.
Orange/amber	2p.m. - 3p.m.
Apricot/tangerine/copper	3p.m. - 4p.m.
Yellow	4p.m. - 5p.m.
Gold (Dusk)	5p.m. - 6p.m.
Blue (Night)	6p.m. - 12p.m.
Green (Emerald)	The midnight hour
Blue (verging on Turquoise)	1a.m. - 6a.m.
Turquoise (Dawn again)	

Celebrate: the action of the Drooma vehicle when it begins to move.

Celebrator: a Droomousine car part.

Chimeroos: small and kangaroo-like, they are terrific hikers. They carry their babies in their brightly colored backpacks, which, soft, comfortable, flexible and compartementalized (for babies, toys and refreshments) are extensions of their backs.

Chromatic diffusion: for the first half of a Glimpsible hour, the sky of Glimpse is diffused by one color, for example from mauve o' clock to mauve-thirty, the sky is completely mauve. For the next half hour, it is increasingly infused by the color of the following hour.

Circumrotating: the head of Gregarious rotates and circumnavigates as he takes in information.

Clawhawks: the scavenger 'watchbirds' of Sooma Sooma.

Clutcher: Droomobile car part.

Colorcollides: found at the Kaleidoshop, they provide startling variations, spectacular transformations, and fleeting, fluorecent illusions.

Color-essence

    Justgimious—red
    Farfetch —orange
    Perceptilly—yellow
    Zippity—blue
    Gumptious—indigo
    Gregarious—Violet
    Spunktaneous—green

Colorhop: popping into color. Glimpsibles are adept at entering the essence of a color.

Comocean: A raging ocean of debris in Sooma Sooma and a color drain.

Concoctic: Farfetch's spontaneous, fantastical illusions.

Crackpotic: Farfetch's spontaneous, fantastical, outlandish illusions.

Crash-landing: occurs when Glimpsibles fail to concentrate when descending from the Any-Colored Sky.

Creamy Memory/Creamoir: Lunaberry Ice Cream contains taste-memories of all the ice creams of the Universe.

Crosscurrents: these angry currents of Comocean thrash, batter, and pummel anyone taking a dip.

Crouch-landing: the best method of landing when soaring, requires bent knees, stiff arms, straight back, and, **intense** concentration.

The Dancing Fountains: one of the Seven Wonders, continually alters the forms, colors and rhythms of their sprayshapements — while whirling and twirling.

Didderdangling: dangling with no plan of action in sight.

Diddler: a Droomousine car part.

Dilemma: an area (state-of-mind) during periods of indecision and confusion. While in this state, options appear equally appealing and unappealing.

Discordance Line: a Drooma Chorus Line—uncoordinated, inharmonious and jarring.

Dizzydazzle: to confuse. While juggling his jugglegems, Spunktaneous confounds the Drooma into deep slumpdumps.

Dizzyswing: an extremely fast action by Farfetch to make him into a Farfetch-go-Around.

Dreamcrash/ing: uninvited invasions into individual or group dreams.

Dream Pillow: soft and comforting, it keeps nightmares at bay.

Dreampool: a sharing of dream-themes. This occurs when Sparks sleepsurge into a common dream.

Dreamscendence/Dreamscending: a transcendental dream experience which transports the Sparks into the whirling colors of their essence.

Dreamsoda: a delicious Lunaberry Ice Cream Soda, with a lingering flavor.

Dredgerlips: the Drooma have lips that extend into cylindrical strawslurps, for draining, swilling, and extracting.

Dripe: a high-pitched combination of tripe and gripe uttred by the Drooma when they are not talking drivel. Dripe is also used as a verb; when Drooma dripe, they grumble, and rumble about tripe.

Drivel: the incessant, senseless twaddle the Drooma utter when they are not talking dripe. Drivel is also used as a verb. Drooma drivel unabated twaddle.

Drooma: who live in Sooma Sooma are jealous, avaricious, hate-filled spectroscopic, color-sucking parasites. They are also lazy, incompetent, inept, clunking, uncoordinated, slow-moving, awkward, and fallibly bad. They are the terror in nightmares, the predators of dreams, who prey on the joy and energy of others.

Droomare: see screammmmmare.

Droomasfear: which surrounds Sooma Sooma and borders the Lumisphere, has a foreboding, enfeebling, depressing, gloomy suction force. Lurking shadows in the Droomasfear are cast by the Droomousine, and indicate a Drooma presence.

Droomousine: the Drooma vehicle and an awful piece of machinery, epitomising Drooma makeshift workmanship. It is an example of the techno-illogical-botchery of the Drooma.

Exceedingly uncomfortable, the Droomousine erupts at destinations causing havoc. Its fumes are offensive.

Droop: the Drooma member of Graball's Droops. Used as a verb, it is what Drooma do when they march.

Droops of Evil: Graball's uncoordinated, drooping troops are the worst army Evil ever had. They droop instead of march.

Dustdumps: the ceiling of the Grudgery has mounds of dust, muck and trash adhering to it.

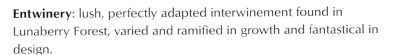

Ellipop: small but elephant-like in shape, this brightly-colored, striped forest creature has a snuffletrunk for sniffing in the past, present and future aromas of Lunaberry Forest and trunkating pop music.

Encyclopediary: is the repository for all learning. Housed in its cavernous foundations, are Justgimious' *One Thousand Facts* — indelibly leaded-in-red (by Fred.)

Entwinery: lush, perfectly adapted interwinement found in Lunaberry Forest, varied and ramified in growth and fantastical in design.

Extrawdite: done through extrawsion.

Extrawsion: removing color-essence is what Drooma like to do to their victims either with their dredgerlips (which become cylindrical strawslurps for sucking and extracting) or by dipping them into Comocean which drains them of color and energy.

Extremulate: elongate and longulate body parts—Farfetch's perfectability.

Evergold: golden plant which arches in Lunaberry Forest.

Factulate: to separate facts from unfacts; truths from fluff.

Factulation: the act of factulating, and the art of separating facts from speculation.

Fantacosmic: cosmic fantasy.

Farfetch-go-Around: through dizzyswinging at enormous velocity, Farfetch becomes a Glimpsible Merry-go-round.

Fizzyfudge: a hot, comforting drink which fizzes with assorted fudge flavors.

Flashdash: extremely fast movement thorugh the Any-Colored Sky.

Flashflourestation: occurs when zigzagging, looping, flashing lights, originating from Farfetch's luminous, orange nose (his illusionator) create a Forest of Light.

Fluctuwaving: The fantastical fluctuations of the wave patterns and movements of the Phantasea.

Fluffifloss: describes the lightweight, frothy, soft, translucent and powdery quality of the clouds in Glimpse.

Fluted-florets: a contributor to Lunaberry Forest orchestrals, these long, slender, fluted flowers make an exquisite high-pitched sound when the breeze rustles through them.

Flutterby Center: the busy Lunaberry Moth market situated in Lunaberry Street, with many storeys spiraling into the sky and stalls clustered on either side of the street.

Flutterhigh Theater: the theater towering above the Flutterby and revolving around it, has an Illusory built for extra-special effects and extravaganzas.

Forest of Light: caused by Farfetch in the Any-colored Sky during shnowwwwtime.

Forethought: a Glimpsible mode of thinking encompassing four phases of forward planning—possibility, probability, particularity, and perfectability—sometimes referred to as "four-thought."

Frolicfly: a playful, translucent fly found in Lunaberry Forest.

Fussflappery: despite their efficiency, the Lunaberry Moths are highly-strung—given to excitability when organizing Glimpsible events, or, when perceiving any reluctance on the part of a Glimpsible to eat what they've prepared.

Ghastlies: occur when the Drooma enter Glimpsible dreams. The Sparks have learned to control their dreams and banish nightmares.

Giroofs: although these eight-legged forest creatures, have very short, stocky multi-colored legs, they still tower over the tallest trees in Lunaberry Forest, and the rooftop of, even, the Flutterhigh Theater, because of their long necks.

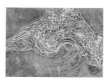

Gloomland: without a glimmer of light, the gloom is so dense that it fogs thought and depresses hope.

Glot/s: measure the intensity of luster, and the passage of time.

Glottery: an abundance of glots.

Glottonous: In huge proportions, for example the extreme fading of a glowessence when glots are gobbled.

Glow: the shine a moodprint gives to color.

Glow-quails: one of the luminous, brightly-colored birds in Lunaberry Forest.

Goldelias: Glittering gold, dahlia-like flowers, growing out of the ochre embankments of Percetilly's Pathway.

Green glowessence: eminates from Spunktaneous, and sparks the green of the rainbow, and the emerald midnight-hour separating the blues of the night.

Greenessence: this is Spunktaneous' essence, his core, his greenicity and potential, which contributes to the completion of the World of Glimpse, that is, sparks Glimpse with bright, emerald green.

Greenicity: Spunktaneous' internal being comes from his greenessence.

Glimpsible Chronicles: containing his daily *Facts of the Day* column, is Justgimious' ongoing, indelibly-written-in-red record of the World of Glimpse, the Glimpsibles, and the Drooma.

Grots: measure length.

Grottage: a measurement in grots.

Grudgery: cavernous, dilapidated accommodation in which Drooma plot, grudge, and dripe.

Headwhizzing Circumrotation: Gregarious' perfectability. He never misses anything relevant or irrelevant when he whizzes his circumrotating head (which continually spins around collecting information of his surroundings in any location).

Hills of Obsolescence: ugly monuments to the Drooma's unselective thievery—mounds of techno-illogical garbage and botchery.

Icicled Memory: Lunaberry Ice Cream contains icicled memories of the flavors of all the ice creams ever created and blended in the Universe, and the frozen-in-time (only happy) emotions of memory associations.

Icedreamery: a bubble-shaped ice cream parlour at the Flutterby Center in Lunaberry Street, where Lunaberry Moths serve Lunaberry Ice Cream (with lingering, metamorphosing after-flavors.)

Illusionator: Farfetch's nose becomes a creative generator and transmitter of illusions during shnnnowwwtime.

Illusory: the stage at the Flutterhigh theater built for extra-special effects and extravaganzas.

Indelible Fact: once they are considered indisputable by Justgimious, these facts are indelibly-written-in-red by Fred (who changes some when Justgimious isn't looking) into the Glimpsible Chronicles or into the cavernous foundations of the Encyclopediary.

Jugglefly: flying and juggling simultaneously is Spunktaneous' perfectability.

Jugglegems: Spunktaneous' precious juggling gems which sparkle, incandesce the sky, and dizzydazzle the Drooma into deep slumpdumps.

Jumpaloon Mountains: one of the Seven Wonders of Glimpse which overlooks the Lake of Imaginings. This mountain range constantly bounces up and down.

Jumpaloon/ing: the act of jumping on Jumpaloon Mountains.

Junk Dump: that's what Sooma Sooma is—the Junk Dump of Infinity—a repository for what has been discarded in the Universe, including the worst of ideas.

Justgimious' Color Theory: Colors are re-creations—products of education and memory, and not an individual's own creation.

Kaleidoshop: walking into this store is like walking into a giant kaleidoscope. The brilliant, flashing, fleeting illusions on its fragmented, mirror-shiny walls, constantly change. All kinds of colorcollides are sold here with startling variations in their tubular and angular transformations.

Kwantifics: within this cubical store at the Flutterby, is an extraordinary selection of sorted, labeled and quantified goods.

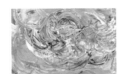

Lake of Imaginings: one of the Seven Wonders of Glimpse where Glimpsibles float and plunge into the depths of their dreams, sometimes merging with other dreamers in a shared unreality.

The Launch of Dawn: an on-the-dot daily occurrence in Glimpse and the precursor of dawn.

Leadache: an ache, generally from fatigue or frustration, common only to Fred the pencil.

Lightlines: glowingly and clearly directs Glimpsibles onto their intrinsic path.

Lightshute: an inclined conduit of bright light down which to slide.

Litter-botched: a landscape rendered ugly by refuse.

Longulated: refers to Farfetch's elongated fingers and his ability to extremulate.

Sparks: There are seven Sensoproblematic Interplanetary Sparks who sense and solve problems and look after Glimpse.

The looooongitudes: are out of Farfetch's sight but within reach of his extending fingers. But as far as Farfetch is concerned, nothing is visually out of reach—only **hard** to reach. His world is full of possibilities—almost within his extennnnsive grasp.

The Lumisphere (Lofty Lumisphere): similar to Earth's stratosphere or ionosphere. Glimpsibles do not generally go there because it is too close to the Droomasfear.

Lunaberries: providing food for both the Lunaberry Moths (who feed at night) and the Glimpsibles (whom the moths feed.) These juicy, translucent, pearl and pink berries are abundant in Lunaberry Forest. They grow all-year round—even peep through pink snow.

Lunaberry Blossoms: these shimmering pink and white blossoms, on which the Lunaberry Moths feed, grow on the Lunaberry bushes and are used by the moths to provide the Glimpsibles with many of their daily needs.

Lunaberry Bushes: found throughout Lunaberry Forest, they are covered all of the year with both Lunaberry Blossoms and Lunaberries—even beneath the pink, winter snow.

Lunaberry Cloths: produced for Glimpsibles by Lunaberry Moths. When worn while soaring in the Any-Colored Sky, these cloths reflect the color of the hour. Worn, when not flying, they reflect the individual's color-essence.

Lunaberry Forest: the dense and magical habitat of the Lunaberry Moths (Forest Arrangers) contain a million species of vegivariation, complex mazes, indigenous flora and fauna such as the Allflower, the Wandering Rootabout and Lunaberry Bushes. Lunaberry Moths feed on the berries and blossoms of these bushes at night and use them for cooking and manufacturing.

Lunaberry Forest Symphony and Orchestra: the sweetest and most mysterious of music emanates from the forest because of the unusual flora and fauna instrumentation.

Lunaberry Ice Cream: available at the Icedreamery, has an after-flavor which lingers and metamorphoses hourly—all day. Within the icicled and creamy memory of one scoop are the collective flavors, consistencies, textures, associated frozen-in-time (only happy) mood-memories of all the ice creams ever created and blended in the Universe.

Lunaberry Moths: these fussy, harassed, maternal moths, with a commercial sense and nurturing instincts, continually flap their brightly-colored wings and mop their brows with their aprons. They are also Forest Arrangers, keeping everything in perfect-growth.

Lunaberry Street: the commercial and entertainment center of Glimpse.

Marshmallow Grass: blue, soft, spongy, and springy.

Marshmallow Grassy Mound: covered by marshmallow grass, they are soft, spongy, springy, and soporific (to Glimpsibles who are sunk-seated). Once powdery blue in color, it will change to blue-emerald-green when Spunktaneous became a Spark.

Matter-of-Factulation: discerning facts from unfacts is Justgimious' perfectability.

Merry-Canary: an extremely cheerful bird in Lunaberry Forest given to raucous laughter as well as the giggles.

Metalustrecology: the study and perception of sheen, luster, and brilliancy—an ability to know a glitter from a glow and all the lusters there are to know. Perceptilly has this gift.

Middler: a Droomousine part.

The Mid-Dot: this dot which separates morning and afternoon, is red, and precedes the red hour when Glimpsibles have their lunch.

Mockery: manifestations of frightening rock-faces of Mount Mockery, representing the fears and vulnerabilities of the victims. The Drooma stage these *mockeries*.

Moodprint: Glimpsibles' individual perception of brightness, influenced by individual emotions.

Morethought: appendixed thought and a Glimpsible mode of thinking is supplemental, but not essential to their main body of instinctive thought.

Mothellaneous: this store in Lunaberry Street contains all the miscellaneous, hard-to-categorize-or-quantify products conceived by the Lunaberry Moths.

Mount Mockery: overlooking Comocean in Sooma Sooma, it infiltrates the minds of victims and becomes the frightening rock faces of internal doubt and fear.

Neverhasdream: a purposely forgotten dream experience, wiped off the map of dreamland.

Neonoptic: Farfetch's glittering, glowing, optical illusions.

Nincomdroops: exceedingly stupid droops.

Numbdumb: mind-numbingly unenlightened.

The Nuse: a teashop in Lunaberry Street (next to the Icedreamery) where Glimpsibles muse while digesting the news—taking each word literally with a pinch (sip) of Lunaberry Tea.

Peep-out and peephole: a window in the ceiling of the Droomousine.

Peppermintdust-wishes: delicious, light, wish-for-more ice cream.

Perceptual Illumination: perceiving the tiniest shadesec (even a split-grot) of difference is Perceptilly's perfectability.

Perfectability: as a result of constantly practicing (and stretching) their abilities, Sparks have attained individual perfectability.

Perfectgrowth: just the right amount of over-and-undergrowth, thanks to the diligence of the Lunaberry Moths, who see to the perfect ecological balance of Lunaberry Forest.

Perfectionnaire: a test devised by Justgimious for apprentice Sparks.

The Perpendicular: a method of climbing rapidly upwards into the sky perpendicularly. Zippity is particularly good at doing this for she has perfected the art of keeping her body as erect, taut, and streamlined as possible, which fascilitates a vertical or angular ascent, followed by a swift descent onto the exact point-of-departure.

Phantaphish: brightly colored, they shimmer with phantom-like transluscency in water, and between rocks and coral.

Phantasea: This ocean, with sparkling-bright colors, and phantom-like wave formations, is home to extraordinary sea creatures such as the **Phantaphish** and the **Twirling-Turtle.** The Phantasea is one of the Seven Wonders of Glimpse.

Point of View: from its multi-angled balconies, Perceptilly teaches "Questions and Reflections"—her favorite subject.

Ponderosity: capacity for deep thought.

Ponderthought: a Glimpsible mode of thought that involves focus and intensity with no distractions.

Ponder-wonder: Thinking intently about something wondrous while, at the same time, pondering the meaning of its being.

Quadruplequick: bounce-walking twice as quickly as running on-the-double, and four times more quickly than a typical walk on-the-single.

Quickety/ies: talking more quickly than thinking. *Verseblurting* is rhyming in quickety style.

Rules of Perpendicularity: very specific guidelines about body posture, observation, and behavior for a Gimpsible doing the Perpendicular.

Rockwriggle: the motion of rocking one's body back and forth, while wriggling it sideways—up, down and all-ways, in order to increase the rhythm and velocity of the bounce-walk.

Rollabout: a rolling, circular motion of the ankles during a bounce-walk in order to increase the swing-spring.

Rotundary: The Sparks round, snug abode.

Sagacity Bush: Justgimious' haven—a comforting, inspiring, all-knowing bush in Lunaberry Forest which helps him factulate.

Screammmmmare: a Glimpsible droomare or nightmare caused by the Drooma.

Sensocosmic head: the rotating head of Gregarious that whizzes round collecting information of his surroundings in any location.

Sensolocational: within certain perameters and in all locations, Farfetch's luminous nose can sense movements and energy. It illuminates the night-sky—and the Glimpsible paths.

Sensoproblematic Interplanetary Sparks: have perfectabilites which help them sense and solve problems.

The Seven Wonders of Glimpse: Justgimious selected these Seven Wonders and has written about them in *The Glimpsible Chronicles*—his ongoing account of all things Glimpsible. The Seven Wonders are: *Jumpaloon Mountains, Whooping Clock Tower, The Dancing Fountains, the Phantasea, the Lake of Imaginings, the Skidslippery Pathways, Lunaberry Forest.*

Shadesec: the colors in Glimpse alter second by second, but it requires an extraordinary color sensitivity (which Perceptilly particularly has) to perceive these minuscule changes.

Shaker: A Droomobile car part.

Simulthought: a Glimpsible mode of thought that allows simultaneous, complete thoughts within the borders of thought-quarters.

Sinkmotion: pertains to the slow, soporific descent into the comfort of a Grassy Marshmallow Mound.

Skidslippery: slippery slopes reflect life's wonder—and pitfalls.

Skidslippery Pathways: one of the Seven Wonders of Glimpse, these mirror-shiny pathways reflect individuals' external appearances, and the internal state of their psyches.

Skydot: miniscule—much smaller than a skyspot into which it transforms.

Skymerge/ing: When Sparks skymerge (soar and merge with the sky) during their own color essence, they are revitalized by an elemental flow occurring from this deep, sensory immersion found in the act of soaring. At such times, it is difficult to distinguish the Sparks from the Any-Colored Sky.

Skyspringers: the luminous skyladder Farfetch creates with his luminous nose during his light shows.

Slaplapping: a combination of the slapping action and lapping sounds of liquid.

Sleeplink: the act of sleeping and focusing on thought.

Sleepmerge/ing: when Sparks sleepmerge, they surge into a common dreampool.

Sleepsurge: a rapid, flowing action of the minds of Sparks during sleep, often resulting in collective sleepmerging and dreaming.

Slumpdump: a very deep sleep; often in a seated, but slumped position.

Shnnnnnowwwws: Farfetch's nose-shows (his nose is an illusionator) include strobefloodery.

Smudgeweeds: found only in Sooma Sooma, ugly and filthy, they smudge-out and strangle any kind of growth in their pathway.

Snoreplot: what Drooma do when they snore and plot at the same time.

Snorerumble: what Drooma do when they snore and grumble at the same time.

Snuffletrunk: the ellipop trunks which are adept at trunkating pop-music, and at sniffing in the perfumes of the past, present and future of Lunaberry Forest.

Sooma Sooma: home of the Drooma, is the litterbotched, junk dump of the Universe. Everything there has been slurped, usurped, appropriated and denigrated by the Drooma.

Spark-ability: Glimpsible Sparks have the ability to illuminate Glimpse with their individual coloressences.

Sparkle-flickers: brilliant, fleeting flashes of color.

Sparkhood: having the essence of perfectablility to be part of the family of Sparks.

Sparkletti: light from the rainbow which dapples luminously over Glimpse.

Sparksplatter: these sparks which splatter the sky when Spunktaneous juggleflies, are a physical manisfestation of his spontaneity and creative spirit.

Spectroscopic parasites: the Drooma who try to extract, suck out, drain and empty all color in Glimpse.

Splashspread Phosphorescence: extraordinary, diffuse, luminous emanations of the Sparks.

Split-grot: even less than a shadesec or a split-second.

Spot-of-Gloom: the warning that the Drooma are approaching.

Sprayshapements: shapes of the spray from the waves of the Phantasea which are immensely varied and surprising in their formation.

Strawslurps: cylindrical in shape and extentions of the Drooma's dredgerlips, they are used for sucking, slobbering and extraction.

Stretcharch: stretching and arching at the same time, like the Rainbow of Glimpse.

Stretchlimbulate: Farfetch stretches his limbs to the ultimate of their tensibility.

Strobefloodery: the auroraborealis of the World of Glimpse which appears in the Any-Colored Sky during dreamscendence time (when Spark Glimpsibles dreamfly in the sky—a transcendental experience).

Stubble-grass: the only kind of grass in Sooma Sooma, it looks like the Drooma's day-old stubble.

Swing-spring: the rhythmic, body motion of the bounce-walk, accelerated by a rolling circular ankle movement and a freeswinging, forward-backward arm motion.

Swiveler: rotating chair found in the Illusory.

Swirlpool: pools of swirling water.

Swoosher: a Droomousine car part.

Swooploop: swooping and looping.

Thinklink: the seamless integration of mind and action, making what Glimpsibles do, seem easy, even though it is not.

Thinkquizziting: thinking and questioning oneself about what one is thinking—an ongoing, internal debate and dialogue.

Thought: Glimpsibles become intensely engaged in thought (housed in their thoughtquarters.) Their modes of thought are: ***beforethought, morethought, forethought, wonderthought, ponderthought and simulthought and afterthought.*** But the highest rung on the Glimpsible thought-ladder is their ability to thinklink.

Thoughtquarters: the residence of Glimpsible thought.

Thoroughfare of Despair: the thoroughness of despair in a Scaremare and at the edge of Mount Mockery.

Thwackers: ten-fingered hands of the Drooma.

Trashburgers: broiled garbage burgers without any food value. Insatiably hungry Drooma (the junk-junkies of the Universe) consume these in great quantities.

Trunkate: an ellipop action of trumpeting pop-music through the snuffletrunk.

Twaire: the vacant stare of the Twoodle-aire.

Twistlanding: an ability to twist and land at the same time.

Twistorting: an extreme distortion often seen in the hideous, jealous, angry, frightening, contorted expressions on the faces of the Drooma, and on the rocks of Mount Mockery.

Twoodle-aire: A feeble-minded bird in Glimpse that spends a lot of time twairing (having the twaires—a combination of staring and not registering) into space. Twairing and twoodle-airing are interchangeable. One can be said to have the twaires or the twoodle-aires.

Upward Perpendiculation: elevating without deviating en route to upward mobility is Zippity's perfectability.

Vegivariation: a huge variation in the vegetation of Glimpse. In Lunaberry Forest, two million species of vegivariation intertwine, and the scents of one million different flowers mingle.

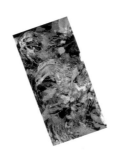

Verseblurt: rhyming on demand almost as quickly as breathing, often used for detailed memorization.

Verseblurt Cafe: where the Sparks meet to versify, verseblurt, have fun, and show off. A social center.

Wall of Olivine: Spunktaneous' wall of defense which emanates from his green-essence. All Sparks have walls of defense of different colors arising from each of their individual essences.

Wandering-Rootabout: capricious, nomadic plant that has a propensity to root and uproot at a whim.

Wanderthought: Glimpsible mode of thinking when their minds wander grots and grots from the source of their original thought.

Waves of Murk: the raging waves of Comocean which dump debris and junk.

Whirlwind of Words: a confused state of mind when words abound but their meanings are unintelligible.

Whooping Clock Tower: one of the Seven Wonders, it whoops joyfully and dances each time the hour changes.

Windtrills: found in Lunaberry Forest, whirl in the wind and sing with crystal clarity.

Wonderthought: A Glimpsible mode of thinking involving a feeling of wonder and awe about what the individual is thinking.

The Yarnspinnery: a factory-store in which Lunaberry Moths spin, weave, chatter incessantly (above the noise of the machines.) They spin and weave all manner of yarnspinnery—from unique mothtiques to tall stories.